# Here We Go Again

# Here We Go Again

V. P. Taylor

First Printing, 2022

ISBN 978-1-951883-76-8

Butterfly Typeface Publishing
PO Box 56193
Little Rock, AR 72215

Dedication

This book is dedicated to the two women

in my life who taught me that a woman's

true strength lies in the way that she loves.

One loved with firmness and dominance,

the other with humility.

I am grateful to both respectfully.

This book is also dedicated to my 3 why's,

that love in action eternally.

*"Sometimes love comes around and it knocks you down, just get back up when it knocks you down."*
Keri Hilson / Neyo - Knock You Down

# Table of Contents


Prologue........................................................17

   (Trinity) Girl's Trip.....................................17

(Truth) A Whole New World ....................26

(Truth) Home Sweet Home ......................28

(Truth) The More Things Change..............33

(Truth) The More They Stay the Same......36

(Truth) Vengeance....................................39

(Trinity) Where Did You Come From?....45

(Truth) Too Late to Turn Back Now ........51

(Truth) Life Goes On ...............................60

(Truth) Mo Money, Mo Problems............68

(Truth) Building An Empire .....................78

(Trinity) On The Block............................91

(Truth) Game Changer ......................... 100

(Truth) Back to Business ....................... 106

(Truth) Business and Pleasure................ 115

(Trinity) A Teenage Love Affair.............................. 133

(Trinity) Rebound.................................................. 142

(Trinity) From Rebound to Wedding Gown ........ 145

(Truth) Plans in Motion...................................... 155

(Trinity) The Truth.............................................. 163

(Truth) Home is Where The Heart Is.................... 176

(Trinity) Ball of Confusion ................................. 198

(Trinity) Bag of Bullshit...................................... 204

(Trinity) Bankruptcy............................................ 209

(Trinity) This House is Not a Home...................... 214

(Trinity) Baby It's Cold Outside ........................... 219

(Trinity) So Why Do You Stay.............................. 231

(Trinity) My World Came to an End ..................... 238

(Trinity) Success.................................................. 243

About the Author................................................ 249

# Foreword

Here We Go Again is another one of those stories. You know, the one about a girl who meets a guy, falls in love with him, and he breaks her heart. This is one of those stories about a girl (a spoiled princess) who falls for a boy (a thug from the other side of the tracks) who loves her deeply. This is one of those stories about friendship, bonds that can't be broken, lives that have been changed, struggles that are won, and lives that are tragically lost. But most of all, this is one of those stories about redemption and how growing up in the 'hood' can be a curse, but also a blessing in disguise.

Back in the 1980's and 1990's many neighborhoods were plagued with drugs and gang violence. There were many parts of town where you simply could not go if you were not from that area. Young children and adolescents had to be watchful, careful of their surroundings, and even mindful of what colors that they wore.

The death tolls in many parts of the United States doubled, even tripled within a few short years. Surprisingly, the deaths were becoming more violent, with the victims and assailants becoming younger and younger. Popular movies like Colors, South Central, and Boyz In The Hood chronicled the street violence and gang wars that we were experiencing. While directors and producers used media to bring attention to a growing epidemic, these movies had somewhat of a cult effect in a lot of smaller communities.

Larger cities like Los Angeles, New York and Chicago saw increased violence. Smaller cities across the US began to mimic the chaos. Small town police forces began to see a rise in gang graffiti, petty crimes, and juvenile offenders.

While I'm sure during this time law enforcement took note of these minor increases, I don't believe anyone was prepared for the hysteria that followed, which basically amounted to generational genocide. Thousands of young black men across the country were losing their lives daily for what seemed insignificant – color.

My small hometown, Little Rock, Arkansas, unsuspecting as it appeared, had it just as bad as the larger cities. The Little Rock scene was chronicled in a 1994 HBO documentary entitled Banging in Little Rock.

Sometimes I sit and think about those days.

*How did we make it through?* I wonder.

How were we supposed to turn out living in times like that? How do you survive violence, brutality, widespread drug use and crime? How do you grow up in the middle of a war zone - The Wild, Wild West - and survive?

For those of us who did, I think more challenging than surviving was the transition. How do you move from a culture of violence to mainstream America?

When I was younger, the older folks used to say, 'You can take the girl out of the country, but you can't take the country out of the girl.' Meaning no matter where you go, there you are, and there is no escaping your past. If this is true, for all of us kids from the hood who are expected to integrate into a society which despises, looks down upon, and simply doesn't understand our communities, what hope is there that we will ever be successful?

You hear about the entertainers and the athletes who make successful transitions, but what about the schoolteachers, the accountants, the law clerks, motivational speakers and so on who came from and survived those urban war zones?

Are they still hood? How did they transition? Is there hope for the future in spite of where we're from? And if so, how do we fit in and still be true to who we are?

My hope is that our experiences (good and bad) can inspire others to understand the complicated circumstances with which many of us from the hood had to cope. I want people to also understand that oftentimes making the transition from hood life to mainstream (two totally different systems and ways of thinking) can be extremely difficult.

But most importantly, I want to offer encouragement to everyone out there who desires a better life. It can be had.

Our stories of joy and pain can offer hope for those who were born in a certain part of town that, not only can life get better, it can also be great!


Signed,
Trinity, the Optimist

Acknowledgment




Thank you to Mr. Truth himself,

or the version of him that I once knew.

Thank you for not only being the inspiration

behind this work of fiction

but also being a huge motivator.

# Prologue
## (Trinity) Girl's Trip

I can still hear their voices in my head.

"Just start writing!" My girlfriends were so demanding.

"But y'all don't understand," I said, defending my lack of enthusiasm to continue the argument. "I don't know how this story is going to end. I don't know what I'm going to do. I'm just confused."

Unrelenting, they persisted. "Just START writing," they repeated with more force.

"Okay. Okay," I said, finally giving in. "But I am going to need you ladies to help me."

"We will!" They declared.

I'm afraid. I don't know the first thing about writing a book, let alone one about my life. About our lives. While I was an avid reader and an excellent English student in grade school, this would definitely be a new endeavor for me.

"Okay, Shera," as my friends and co-workers affectionately called me, "you can do this. You've dealt with worse and besides there may be other young ladies out there who have been through similar experiences, who are looking for hope and inspiration. Stop being so selfish, Trinity, and write the damn book already!"

Although I remember the conversation with my three best girlfriends like it was yesterday, it was actually the first weekend in March of 2013. We were on a girls' trip to visit and reconnect.

Candace was my childhood friend. She grew up just a few blocks up the street from my home. We had been friends since Rightsell Elementary School, 4th grade. Candace was my twin spirit - very feisty, outgoing, and talkative. We clicked almost immediately and formed a bond that I wouldn't begin to understand until almost 30 years later. Now married with children, she lives in Charlotte.

Well, let me reverse that order so as not to confuse the story later.

Like myself, Candace had children first, moved to Charlotte, where she met a wonderful guy whom she married, and is still married to today (toot toot).

--------

See, I need to make that distinction for you readers to understand how for many people in my life (including myself), the child comes first and marriage second (if at all). But we'll discuss that later in the book.

Up until 2012, I hadn't seen or communicated with Candace in almost 20 years. I thought about her often and from time to time would ask a few relatives of hers about her. I got the same response each time,

"She's married and in Charlotte."

While other cultures offer much detail to a personal inquiry about a person, for us (hood girls), just to know that we are alive and well is enough. Anything more than that just means people are in your business unnecessarily.

Hood 101: Mind your own business!

So, the standard answer of Candace being married and in Charlotte was enough for me. I knew she was fine.

Jewells, who accompanied me on this girls' trip, has been my best friend since the seventh grade. We went to Horace Mann Junior High together. Jewells also stayed in my neighborhood, around the corner from my house. Unlike Candace, Jewells was my opposite. We had a yin/yang type of relationship. We balanced one another out. I was the wild and crazy one. She was more cautious and reserved. Jewells was the good girl in the neighborhood. Her family was religious, and her momma didn't play that! She didn't have as much freedom as I and Candace had, to roam and explore our environment, but at the end of the day, you live where you live, and no matter how reclusive you may be, the hood takes its toll.

Jewells and I have always had an off again, on again relationship, particularly during adulthood. We never really broke up or fell out. We just sort of drift apart and then magically drift back together. When we get back together, it's like a day has never passed. There is a naturalness about our friendship. It is calming and soothing like healing waters. I never imagined us losing friendship, no matter the space between us or the passage of time. I guess with some people, it's just like that. So, prior to 2012 it had probably been a year or so since I had talked to her, and probably five or more years since we had been in consistent contact.

It's amazing how life brings you full circle.

Now days, if I go more than a day without contact from Jewells, we're both sending out search parties!

My girl, Dee (short for Denise), joined us on our reunion. Dee's been my ride or die friend for the last ten-plus years. I met her as an adult; a Christian and a fully-resurrected, fully-integrated-into-society adult. She's never really known the hood side of me, although I have never hidden who I am past or present. Dee is funny, sweet, and sensitive. It's like if you cut her in the middle, warm apple pie filling would flow out. She's not rough around the edges at all.

Now don't get me wrong. She's no Southern Belle either. Dee has some spunk about herself and can get rowdy if she needs to. Dee lives in Little Rock and has consistently, for the last 16 years or so, but admits that this is the longest she has ever stayed in one place.

The youngest of three girls, she was raised by a single mom. Dee's mom often moved from state to state to provide better opportunities for her daughters. Dee didn't experience the neighborhood like we did growing up because her family was often in transition. You could view her childhood as positive (lacking the violence) or negative (instability), but one thing I see is that all that moving around helped her develop adaptation skills. Dee can monitor and adjust better than most people I know, which makes her and my relationship work.

Me? As I said earlier, I am what I would consider flighty, but in a bold kind of way. At any given point I have a million ideas running through my head. I'm a thinker. Notice I said, thinker and not planner. My mantra would probably be 'the devil is in the details.'

As a thinker, I come up with all of these creative ideas, and then I just do them. Sometimes I think it through and sometimes I just take a blind leap of faith (sort of like with this book). When I think too long, I can literally drive myself crazy.

It's almost as if I'm on a cliff and I just decide to jump! Then either one of two things can happen: I can spread my wings and soar, or I can crash and burn. I'm often willing to crash and burn, which has landed me some great successes but also some tough failures.

This is what I call flighty.

But others view me with awe. They say I'm bold, courageous, a go-getter, xyz. I don't get caught up in what I am, but I do know how I function and while it feels crazy at times, it seems to work for me.

All my life I have felt different, called and unique. And all my life I have fought that feeling. I really wanted to be part of the crowd, like all my peers and family. In many ways I was, but in so many other ways I was different.

I was an introvert/nerd who loved learning, knowing, exploring. I was excited by new knowledge and information. I was really bright. Teachers and adults took notice of me early on.

I lived in the hood (as it became known), but I was raised in a loving family. My mom and dad were both me and my older brother's biological parents. My parents were both college-educated, raised in two-parent homes, and earning decent livings. I realized early on that our family was an anomaly in our community. We were the exception rather than the rule.

It felt strange that I had my dad at home, when so many of my friends didn't. I used to think my life was harder than my friends because I had two parents to answer to, instead of one. Little did I know or understand how fortunate I was at that time.

My mom worked for the State and had a good paying job, and my dad was an educator. Our home was stable, and we were pretty spoiled as kids, by the standards of those times. I had no idea of what life was really like for my friends and neighbors. In my mind, we were all just living, and we were all equal. I didn't realize then how much of an advantage having both parents who had already fully transitioned into mainstream America gave me.

So here we all were: Candace, Jewells, Dee, and me having a reunion right here in Charlotte, North Carolina. Reminiscing about the good ole days and thankful that we made it out okay without losing life or limb.

I saved a lot of our old pictures from childhood. I keep them by my bed to remind me from whence I came. Sometimes things happen in life - things that can't be explained - and you have to go back to move forward. That's what 2012 was like for me - a blast from the past that brought me here with my girls to take a second look at our childhood, with wiser eyes.

The strange thing about memories is how we frame them. Some of us only put the good thoughts from the past in our mental frame, and some of us only the bad. It's not until that past comes knocking at your door that you must face your truths; the good, the bad and the ugly.

Prior to 2012, I was what most would consider successful. I finished both my undergraduate and graduate degree by the time I turned 25. I was a licensed mental health therapist. I had held administrative positions in mental health clinics and began a private practice with three other colleagues in 2010. I have served on boards, taught at the University where I am an alumnus, and conducted trainings and seminars. That flightiness paid off, because I've accomplished a lot in a few years.

I know that the Lord has been with me, guiding me and sustaining me, because when I look at my past, I know that I couldn't have done it on my own. As a matter of fact, no matter how much I accomplish I cannot seem to let go of who I used to be. Sometimes when I sit in important meetings, with important people, I think, *these people really don't know me. I bet they have no idea some of the things I've had to overcome. More importantly, I bet they don't even care, and here I sit right next to them.*

People see the resurrected me and they praise her, but would they feel that way if they had known me B.C. (Before Christ)? Same thing goes for church folk. I'm an upstanding member of my community. I own a business. I've been married to the same man for 15 years. All of my children are by him. Would they be interested to know that our oldest is 17 (do the math)? I had her when I was that same age.

See, no matter how others view me, I know myself and I accept myself - all of me. I don't get caught up in the hype because people can only break you if you let them. Staying this close to the ground helps me keep my footing. I've been living and doing fairly well, but for years I have felt out of place, like I have been transported from a life I knew to an unfamiliar one.

Yes, I'm successful, but I don't truly feel at home. I almost feel fake. Like a phony. I mean I know that I am a multifaceted person. I embrace my inner nerd.

But what happened to that little hood girl, who was also so much a part of me and who I was? Did I bury her? And if so, is that what I'm promoting to all of the girls I've worked with throughout the years?

If there is something that you don't like about yourself, just bury it and hope it never finds you again. For years, this method worked for me.

I was successful, until ...

V. P. Taylor

## (Truth) A Whole New World

I've done the same thing, the same way for the last 14 years: Wake up at 5:00 am. Drink coffee and wait 30 minutes for the Correctional Officer (C.O.) to unlock my door. Breakfast at 6:00, school at 7:30, and back to the unit to watch ESPN and ESPN2 until 10:30. Lunch is at 11:00 and then basketball from 12:00 pm until 3:00 pm.

I go through the same things every day. Every day is the same way.

My name is Tyreque Robinson, but everyone calls me Truth. I'm an inmate at FCI (Federal Correctional Institution), Forrest City, Arkansas. I have been here since January 20, 1998.

I'm on my way to the basketball court with my homies. The loudspeaker announces:

"Tyreque Robinson. Report to R and D."

Turns out I'm being released ASAP due to a new law that has to do with the disparity between crack and powder cocaine.

I report to the R and D (register and deliver) Unit and find my Counselor, Mr. Gilmore there.

"Pack your shit, Mr. Robinson," he says smiling at me. "You're going home and frankly we will not miss you around here. Now hurry up. You have to be off this compound before the 3 o'clock count."

Now being as though I have been in this dump for more than 13 years you know I'm ready to get the fuck from around here. And I simply won't miss none of the motherfuckers in here either. Shit, I didn't even have to pack.

"Y'all can have all this shit," I told my cellmate and a few other good men. "My cellmate will hold it for you until you come get it."

I did the prison handshakes and gangsta hugs and was soon walking down the street towards the bus station with my pictures, a few letters, and a long-ass piece of paper with a gang of phone numbers on it.

I'm looking around at everything. I'm taking in the sights.

It's like a whole new world to me. I have been locked up since I was 19 years old. It's November 2011. I am a grown-ass 33-year-old man who doesn't even know how to use a cell phone.

V. P. Taylor

# (Truth) Home Sweet Home

I walk into my grandmother's house, and it look just as it did the day I walked out. Food is cooked and my great grandmother and the rest of my family are there and it's the best day of my life. All of my little cousins, nephews and nieces are there too. I feel this little tug on the back of my shirt, and I turn around and here is this little fly ass nigga standing there. All four feet of him is looking up at me.

"My name is Lil Tim," he says, "and we need to talk 'cause I been getting into trouble."

Everyone in the house starts to laugh 'cause lil' man is dead ass serious. I snatch him up into my arms.

"Who does this lil guy belong to?" I ask.

Me, my family, and some of my friends spend the day talking. As the day slowly starts to turn into night things start to move outside.

My best friend, Lil Dink, hands me some money and asks, "What's next Big Homie?"

"Shit bro, I'm just going to take it slow," I tell him, "get a job and just try to get relaxed and enjoy my family for a while you know?"

"Yeah, I can dig it bro," he says. "But in the a.m. I'm coming to get you so I can show you the town and get you a few things".

"Ok," I say. And bro bounces out.

My little cousin Kayla comes outside.

"Can I use your car?"

"Yea," she says and hands over the keys to her blue Chevy Trailblazer.

I'm listening to Lil Boosie's Bankroll, riding through my old neighborhood looking at all the old places I used to go. I even bumped into a few of my old friends, still looking the same - doing the same shit that they were doing when I left thirteen years ago.

------

The next day Lil Dink (aka Dinky) came to pick me up.

"I'm taking you shopping," he said.

We went to a spot called S. Dot Urban, where we met a guy named Johno. Dink told him my story.

"This the big homie," Dink told Johno. "Remember his name and face."

He took me to the back of the store, and it was like fashion heaven: Gucci, RR, TR, Robin Jeans, POLO, and a gang of other named brand fashions. Bro spent like $4,000.

"Next stop, the mall and then City Gear," Dink told me.

I went Jordan and Air Malcolm crazy. Another $2,000 in shoes and I was set.

After that we went to his house where I met Lil PJ, Trent, Lil T, Odie Wane, Big T and a few other niggas. It was Bloods and Crips in there, but it was like one big family. Anyway, shit started moving fast after that.

We ended up in the Paper Moon, a strip club off Mabelvale Pike. We were having drinks and shit was going good. We had a table for like eight and my home boy told two beautiful bitches that I was fresh out of prison and that I had did 14 years and haven't had no pussy yet. They was all over me in seconds asking questions, one was black and the other one white but both were clearly the baddest two bitches in the Moon.

That night was my first threesome, and I was instantly turned out. I went through like, seven gold packs. The white girl had fallen asleep, but the other girl kept asking me questions.

"Didn't you just come home?"

"Yea, why?"

"Cause you still going nigga. My pussy hurts," she shouted. "That's why!"

I was turned all the way up.

The next morning, I woke up freshly fucked and ready to go see my family. I had been out four days, and they had only seen me for a few hours. Plus, I needed to go see my P.O. (parole officer) by noon. I make it to the house, kiss my G lady, tell my mother that I'm ok and that I was at Dink's house.

I jump in the shower and get myself together and call Dink to come take me to see my P.O. When he pulls up, he's in this all red Charger with red rims on that bitch. It's clean as hell, but it's red. This nigga jumps out blued up from the shoes up.

"Boy, what you doing in this loud MF?"

He just laughs and says, "This my baby momma shit," and introduces me to Ann.

"Shit nigga you can't talk," he says, "wait till you see your baby momma. Her shit is just as loud."

We laughed and pulled off headed for downtown Little Rock so that I can check in with them people. My P.O. is this young black lady named Ms. Dabney and she looks cool enough, but as soon as she opened her mouth, I knew I was in trouble!

"So, Mr. Robinson. I see you used to be in a gang," she says. "Are you still active?"

"No," I said looking her right in the eyes.

"Well," she says staring right back at me, "I'm just going to tell you right now that these folks are not playing with you. They want your ass in a sling right next to your big brother

Leeland Robinson. So, you had better not be fooling around with the set."

I just sit there and continue to look at her.

"Where are you living?" She asks. "Who else lives there? What kind of car do you drive?"
She asked all kinds of other bullshit ass questions. It took about two hours, and finally I was able to go, but she made sure that I knew how to use this coded phone shit where I have to call in every day and listen for my color to see if I've got to come in for a urine test.

*This shit is crazy,* I thought. But I'm glad to be free, nonetheless.

Shit is going good. I got a BAR-B-Q set up for the weekend in the park in the old neighborhood. Everything is set up nice and smooth, and by now the word is out: one of the 23rd Street OGs is out and having a cookout in the park.

## (Truth) The More Things Change

Back in the day before I went to prison, it was too hard to go out in Little Rock if you was Cripping. The town is just too full of Bloods. For every Crip there's at least five or six Bloods. So, when we would go out to parties and clubs or even to the mall on the weekends, a nigga gots to be strapped up and ready to blast that thang. It was bound to go down whenever, however, and wherever.

The city ain't like that no more, so nigga is kicking it like a motherfucker all over the place.

I'm going out so I call my nigga and let them know what's up, but they get back and say, "Don't go this weekend, we will go out Christmas weekend and shut the city down."

----------

It's December 17, 2011 and I've been out a little over a month. I got this fine ass chick that I was going to meet up with. I was trying to get my dick wet as much as I could (fourteen years is a long ass time, you know), so me and my nigga Lucky fall up into this club called La'Changes on Roosevelt Road, right across the street from the county jail. It's packed like a motherfucker, and of course I'm blue down and my lil nigga Luck is on flame.

We go to the bar and get drinks, I see a few faces that I know, head nods are given and a few pounds here and there, as me and my lil nigga moving through the club.

He spots some nigga that he knows, leans in and tells me, "Keep ya eyes open Unc, it might be about to get real."

I'm like, "With who?"

He tells me that its a few nigga that him and Dinky been beefing with for a while, but every nigga in this bitch looks alike to me. I know none of these lil nigga, but as shore as shit stank, like, five niggas walk up and say something to Lucky. He tells them to keep on pushing 'cause they don't want these troubles. I'm pulling nephew along and the niggas keep coming.

One got a lil too close and before I know it Lucky is smashing the nigga in the face with a glass bottle, now we're fighting like a motherfucker. The bouncers get us broken up and push me and Lil Bro outside.

I call Dinky just to tell him that me and Luck just got through squabbling with some nigga, and he says, "What! Who? Stay right there. I'm on my way!"

It's like five minutes pass and Dinky, Scooter, Odie Wane and Lucky pull up. We are right back into the club knocking out bouncers and niggas along the way. Uzo in the lead and I'm right on his heels. Now it's one big ass fight, motherfuckers running and screaming and then I hear four gunshots, bang, bang, bang, bang!

The lights come on and the crowd gets cleared, and I see my nigga on the ground shot. I fall there beside him and hold his head in my lap.

He was already gone.

V. P. Taylor

## (Truth) The More They Stay the Same

And just like that, I'm right back in it.

My best friend and brother died in my arms just thirty-three days home after doing thirteen and a half straight years in prison! What a welcome home.

The next morning my mother is waking me saying, "Truth, you need to get all these people out of my yard!"

I'm like, "Who are you talking 'bout ma?"

I walk to the front door and look outside, and it looks like the whole neighborhood is in our yard, only this time it's a bunch of hurt and very angry 23rd Street Crips! I tell them to go in the back yard, and I go to the bathroom to brush my teeth and wash my face. I then put some clothes on, and my mother pokes her head into my room and just looks at me for a few seconds. Then she says, "Baby be careful."

At this point I have so many thoughts running through my head, first I'm thinking about my nigga and his family. He had two beautiful little girls, his mother and his sister. Then I'm thinking about smashing on the fools who are responsible for all of this bullshit, and all I can say to myself is, *Truth, you just came home.*

I walk into my mother's kitchen and hug her.

"I love you Ma," I hug her. "You know I'm going to be ok."

And with that I head out the door to go and address this angry mob of killers in my mother's back yard. They are ready to raise the crime rate around here. There had already been three or four different stories of what happened at the club last night. My niggas know that I was there and that I'm gone give it to them uncut and straight to the point.

One version of the story is that the DJ played Piru Love, and that the fight started from there. Another version of the story said that Dinky got into it with someone over a bitch. The last story was so far out that I simply refuse to mention it.

I give my niggas the run down and then, "Don't yall come back to my mom's house like this no more. Mannie and C-boy, yall stay back."

I tell them that I will contact them and gave instructions to tell the rest of the homies to be on standby, that way we never have to be one hundred deep at my mom's shit again. They start leaving two and three at a time. C-boy and Mannie are the last two to go.

Finally, I am alone with my thoughts.

Deep down I know that all the shit I was telling myself in prison about not getting back in the gang life had just flown right out the window.

I'm back, and all it took was thirty-three days, and the life of one of the realest nigga I had ever known, to help me make up my mind.

I say a silent prayer for my homie and then I promise him that bodies are going to drop all over the city behind him.

## (Truth) Vengeance

The first thing I do the next day is call Lucky, because I'm sure he knows the niggas from the club, who they are and what they look like. Plus, he's a young nigga and is with the shit, so I know that he can get us some heat.

We go to a barber shop in West Little Rock. I'm thinking he's trying to get a fresh line or something, but when we walk in no one else is there but an old cat name Lou.

Luck walks up to Lou and says, "This is Truth, Dinky's big bro that I told you about."

The old man looks at me and nods for us to follow him. We go down into what looks like a basement. When he turns on the lights, it looks more like a gun store. I'm looking around at guns that I have never seen before in my life. I'm talking some real heavy shit. But the old man keeps walking, so we keep following him until he tells Luck to wait outside the door.

We are in a small room and it's just a table and two chairs. He sits and motions to the other chair for me to have a seat. He tells me that Dinky was like the son that he never had and that he loved him very much. He says that he would still be alive if I had not made that phone call (damn) and that Dink owed him $65,000 and that that debt is now mine.

He told me that he knows I had just come home from federal prison and that I don't have any money, but he is willing to overlook the debt for now, until I can get on my feet enough to pat it.

I'm like, I don't know how I'm going to come up with that kind of money (damn again).

He asks me what I planned on doing to the people responsible for killing my brother and his son?

I just looked at him, 'cause I don't know this guy, but I trust Lucky with my life, so I feel like he would not bring me here unless he knew we need this old man. And seeing those guns up front, I know he has something that I want.

I made lil bro a promise.

Lou gives me a cell phone and tells me that the number that is programmed into it can reach him at any time of the day or night. He tells me that me and Lucky can pick any weapon we want off that wall. He tells me to call him in one week and we will talk a lil bit more. I tell him ok and we go back out and get Luck. We head back to the wall full of guns.

It's crazy, cause I know that I am about to take steps into the game that I can never take back. But hey, this is the life that has been chosen for me and I plan on living it a long ass motherfucking time!

With that thought I take two FN57's off the display and ask for two extra magazines and two boxes of ammo. Each magazine holds twenty-two 5.62mm rounds. Lucky grabs the same. Lou gets our orders together for us and tells me that the weapons and ammo are gifts from him to me and a token of future business together.

Once we walk outside, I ask Luck what was that all about? He tells me that Dinky was waiting for me to get out and planning for me to meet Lou anyway, 'cause he knew that I could handle whatever Lou puts in my hands. He said that Bro had already told Lou about me, and he had had plans for Lou and me to hook up.

So, in a sense, Lou has been waiting on me as well. He had been trying to get Dinky to move up, but he didn't want to handle no more than what he was already getting, which was about 150 pounds of popcorn.

I take that all in, then I ask lil Bro, "So where these niggas be at? Let's go show them that Lil Bro can reach out and touch they ass from the afterlife!"

Lucky looks at me and says, "They told me that you was a monster with that hammer, but I think you are washed up." I just smile and tell him to lead the way.

We rode all over - Little Rock, North Little Rock, Jacksonville, all over John Barrow, the west side, the south side. We had been looking for them clowns all day since about 11:00 a.m.

We were coming from the south on our way to southwest Little Rock, going the back way down Arch Street, when I thought about this little food spot called Brewster's Place, that my baby momma had been telling me about. I'm starving like shit, so I tell Lucky to make that stop. We are like two blocks away. When we pull in looking for a place to park, lil bro hits me in the chest and says, "Unc that looks like one of them nigga's cars right there."

At that point the door to Brewster's opens up and out walks three lil dudes, and Luck is like, that's them, that's them!

They are not paying us any attention, so I tell Lucky to make a block and I get out. He pulls off and I walk straight at them, thinking that 'cause I'm fresh out of the feds, they won't know my face. Wrong!

One of them is talking on a cell, the other is looking at his phone, and the last one is looking at me with wide open eyes, like he knew what time it was. He couldn't say shit 'cause the other two never saw what hit they bitch asses.

I was shooting from the hip and unloading on all targets.

With my guns smoking, I walked right out into the middle of the street and got into the car as Luck slowly pulled off down Arch Street.

We were driving down the street doing the speed limit and not saying a word. Finally, Lucky sneaks a peek at me and says, "Fuck and monster Unc, you a motherfucking beast that should've never been let out of the cage. But I'm glad I'm on your side, 'cause these niggas out here is in trouble."

I look back at lil bro and say, "I'm hungry fool. Can we stop somewhere and get something to eat please?"

After we get a bite to eat bro tells me that he got to ditch the car and take care of some other business. I have him drop me off at my brother B.D.'s house. Big bro is sitting outside drinking Bud Lights out of the can and talking shit to his main man Double D.

He says, "What's up lil bro? I heard bout Lil Dink. I know that shit caught you off guard and I'm sorry for your loss."

I tell him yeah and thanks, then I ask can I go get a nap on the sofa. When I wake up, its 8:57 pm and the Fox16 news is coming on in three minutes. I think all hood niggas watch the news whenever we get a chance. Low and behold, breaking news:

*A triple homicide at Brewster's place in the parking lot this evening and police have no suspects, except a black male was seen walking to a white convertible mustang and getting in on the passenger side and slowly pulling away. The one witness could not give a positive ID on the license plate.*

My brother and D looked at me like, 'ain't that the same kind of car that dropped you off earlier?'

I don't say shit, and they just look at each other, shake their heads and leave me alone.

# (Trinity) Where Did You Come From?

It was a mild December day in 2011, my business partner and I were out to lunch discussing the transitions for the approaching new year.

As decided upon when we first opened our practice, we would each serve two years as the Director of our company, with me taking the first two with initial startup. I was moving into year two of my tenure and lining out the upcoming year of transition.

Now I know I described myself as flighty, I think I should interject here, but not when it comes to business. When it comes to business, 'I'm 'bout that life!'. As we're sitting in the restaurant talking shop, my peripheral view sees what appears to be a ghost. No, not really a ghost, but from my reaction and response it might as well have been. I was stunned, to say the least.

The professional banter that I was engaged in came to a halt, I could not speak, my skin became flushed and butterflies were celebrating the end of the Civil War in my stomach.

I know this is not who I think it is, because if it is I'm dead, figuratively speaking. It has to have been at least 20 years since I have seen, talked to or been in contact with him.

*And what the hell is going on with me right now, why am I responding in this way? I'm a therapist for Pete's sake!*

As soon as he walked through the door, I knew who he was, and that was from a peripheral view. Not once did I make eye contact with him. Hell, I couldn't. I was scared. Why? Of what? I'm a grown-ass woman. Why on earth am I afraid? I can't think of the last time I've been scared like this.

Actually, prior to this encounter, I don't ever remember feeling this way before. I'm a bold person, I help people, I speak before groups of people, I'm a business owner, educated, a Christian. And yet, none of those things are helping right now, at this very moment.

My partner, Misha, is looking at me in bewilderment because in all the years that she's known me, I'm sure she's never seen this much emotion out of me. If I could have gotten up from the table and run without it being really noticeable, I would have, but I couldn't, so I just sat.

Meanwhile, as I'm having a supernatural experience on one side of the restaurant, he is on the other side. Just as paralyzed, I'm assuming.

I later concluded this because he sat down and sent his friends over to talk to me. How funny, now, but at the time I was in no mood for laughter. I knew one of his friends. I had gone to high school with him. But I didn't know the other guy. I don't remember much except that I was praying for them to leave.

I don't like my feelings. We are not friends, and I sure am not comfortable sharing them with others. In my hood, showing too many feelings was a sign of weakness that could have dire consequences. Feelings made you weak, a victim, and I was taught to 'tuck your feelings in your pocket.'

It's not that you don't have feelings, you just don't deal with them. You keep it moving.

Now in the therapeutic world, this is a direct contrast to what I was taught. In the therapeutic world you embrace your feelings. Well, if that scenario was a lesson in embracing my feelings, I was ill-prepared and failed miserably.

Not only could I not embrace them, I couldn't shake them, move, or speak.

Eventually, he left.
Long after he left, long enough that I could be sure there was no chance of bumping into him in the parking lot, I was able to halfway explain my response to Misha and leave the restaurant.

It took me the greater part of the rest of the week to process that encounter.

I finally chalked it up to a small personal lesson, or a glance into where I was and who I am. I'm raising a teenage daughter, and empathy is always a good thing to have, right? I couldn't have been more wrong.

Somehow in the back of my mind I knew that that would not be the last time I'd have to face my past. To face him. But as we humans do, we often fool ourselves into a state of well-being.

We get up, we keep at our jobs, our families, our lives. We don't take out time to deal with things or to deal with ourselves. We keep moving until we are forced to face those difficulties. Some call it hitting a brick wall. I like to think of it as an awakening.

The lives that we just trudge along in are almost like sleep walking. We are almost in a trance, then something happens, often something tragic, and we wake up!

Well, back in December, I woke for a little moment and hit the snooze button. It wasn't more than several months later that I had to answer the alarm.

--------

I've worked all across my city, particularly with youth in the more urban 'hood' schools.

I knew when I began college that I wanted to give back to my community. I wanted to work with youth, to help others find a way out of dysfunction and poverty, to use the skills that the streets provide you with, and to adapt them and make them profitable in the mainstream.

I always knew that I could succeed, even during those times that were most challenging. I knew that I would. One of my co-workers calls me the 'Harriet Tubman of the Hood'. I think that's cute, but it does hold some truth regarding my philosophy of how I should function in society.

Once I found my way out, I knew I'd be remiss if I didn't help others. That would seem ungrateful and unappreciative to me. So, since I completed grad school in 2004, I have been on a mission. I have been able to connect with and assist so many kids because I know that deep within me, I am them. I may not be engaged in some of the things they are into, but at the core, we are all at some point victims or victors of our circumstances.

The question becomes how can I be the latter rather than the former? Because I have first-hand experience, I can relate, teach and lead, and I have. I'm not proud about much, but when it comes to the work I've done with the kids, I am proud not only of myself, but of them as well.

Now, not all of the kids that I have worked with have done well. Some still struggle, but the majority are still in the game. Every time I'm out and see one of my former students, I am proud of them. They recognize me in stores and restaurants, and that makes me proud that I've been able to impact their lives. Some of my former kids are now adults who still stay in touch to get advice or use me as a referral, or just to keep me updated on their progress. Just as fate would have it, one of those kids is related to him. I didn't immediately make the connection, but maybe a year or so into knowing each other, she mentioned who her family was.

Immediately I remembered her. I had to be about thirteen or fourteen years old during that time, and she was a cute little curly headed chocolate girl, no more than two or three years old.

Even with that discovery, I knew that he was away and had been for some time. This was probably in 2007. I asked about him a few times but we had no serious conversations about him. I didn't let her know that we had dated when I was younger.

So, when she reached out to me in July, the significance of his reappearance dawned on me.

## (Truth) Too Late to Turn Back Now

It's been two weeks since the club shooting and the triple homicide at Brewster's Place, and things are moving way faster than I thought. I have talked with Lou over the phone once and had more than a few sit downs, and come to find out, Lou is Dinky's Godfather. He and Dinky's father were good friends back in the day, and they were both in the Army together when bro's dad was killed. He only had one son, and asked Lou to always be there for him. Lou was always a man of his word, as well as a man of respect, and he was doing just that.

He told me that Dinky told him all about me, and said that lil bro really had big plans for us once I got out. Lou also said that he sees no reason why we can't still make lil bro's vision real. He told me that lil bro's debt was forgiven 'cause he went by lil bros house, and the work was still there. It had not been touched. It was counted and put into the stash. He gave me the work and it was 150 pounds at $44,000, that's 400 a slab, and I'm dumping the whole # on one nigga in Conway for $700 a slab.

So, as you can see, shit is looking real good right about now. I had an old school Monte Carlo out at my aunt's house in the country in Wrightsville, so I went and got it, slapped some 24" IROCZ on that bitch, painted it black and didn't look back.

Lucky called, "You going out tonight?" He asked me.

"I don't know," I told him, "cause I got a Bar-B-Q in the hood in the AM, and that's going to be an all-day event."

I went all out for the first 23rd Street. Day with the help of a few good men and women. Mike Jones was on the grill. He works for Budweiser, so the beer was plentiful, plus we all came together on all the food and other shit. Jannie is like the hood mother. We can't get shit done without her and the lady Locz. They have to contact the city so that we can block off the street. They're the ladies that plan and make shit happen!

The home boy Ron is on the set in full swag, and his wife made sure that some of her home girls showed up. It's a beautiful Sunday afternoon, and I can just feel that it's going to get better. We have plenty food and drinks, and of course that good loud smoke is in the air.

I'm really having the time of my life looking out over the park from the tower. It feels good to see all my home boys and home girls having a good time and enjoying themselves. I just wish that Dink BKA Dinky was here to see this shit.

While I'm sitting off to the side in the tower, my cousin James come up and says, "Cuzz, it's a little bad ass bitch out there with Ron's wife and she got some sexy ass tatts on her thighs, she said she looking for the nigga that drive the black old school."

I'm like, "Yeah let me check this shit out."

If you know anything about me then you know I swear I'm a lady's man.

Me and Cuzzo walk out of the tower and down the steps and I'm like shit, but I don't show it. Every real player must have a mouth full of poker chips and a smooth poker face to match it, but this lil motherfucker is fine, maybe five foot two and thick as a bucket of blood, with some dukes on that's short as hell and the pussy is on straight blast. And she got cat paws running up her legs.

This lil chick is bad for real, so I'm looking her up and down and say, "Who wants to know who's driving the old school?"

"Trice wants to know," she says, "cause he's blocking me in. I'm trying to leave to go get something from around the corner at Ron's house."

I have to think fast, 'cause this is one that I gots to put on the team, so I toss her my keys and say, "Go ahead."

Before she can refuse, I turn and walk back up the steps.

See, this buys me some time. Either she gone just go around there in my car, which if she do that, by the time she gets back and have to bring me my keys, I will have a game plan. But if she don't drive my car, by the time she catches up to me to tell me she ain't driving my car, I will at least be out of sight of everyone else, and I'll have to try my hand and shoot straight from the hip.

Either way I'm getting that phone number. When she didn't come up behind me, I knew I had her, 'cause last but not least, she gone need me to flip the kill switch for the car to even start.

I tell Cuzzo, "I'll be right back," and I run down to my car. As she is turning the key, I hear her saying something bout my shit being a fancy hunk of junk.

I say, "My bad baby, I forgot to tell you about the kill switch." I flick it and my bay jumps right over! Then I say, "Don't be joy riding in my shit."

And she says, "Ride with me."

So, I jump in, and we go.

She says, "Damn your car rides so smooth."

I tell her thanks and then I say fuck it and go for the kill shot.

"What are you and me doing tonight and where are we going?" I ask her.

"You don't even know my name."

"You already pushing my whip." I come back.

"Well, my name is Trice. Yours is Truth, and it's up to you, baby, on what we do for the rest of the day and night."

In my head I'm saying check mate!

Trice runs in and uses my home boy's bathroom and comes back out and asks for my phone, which I hand to her and watch as she programs her number, then takes a picture of herself and puts it so when she calls the pic shows up. We get back to the park and everybody is looking at us as we walk up. My home girls are shaking their heads at me, and I'm looking like, "What?"

But really, it was a beautiful day, and I must say the first 23rd Street Day ever was a success.

After everyone leaves, I make sure that all the trash is picked up, the grills are returned to their rightful owners, and I tell the homies that I am going to climb the Hill (a premier night club) tonight. I then call Trice and tell her that I'm going home to change clothes and get fresh, and that around twelve, I'm going on the Hill. She says she will meet me there.

I walk into the house and my BM is about to go straight postal on my ass.

"Who was the bitch driving your car, huh Tyreque?"

I'm like, "Dude, wasn't no bitch driving my car. What are you talking about?"

"Why you lying, hunh Tyreque? Christy's cousin's baby momma said some light skinned bitch was driving your car about an hour ago."

So just to get her off my back, I made up a fast one and said that was Ron's wife. Her car got blocked in, and you know how females don't like using public restrooms, so I let her run around the house to pee.

Bam! Shut that shit down just like that!

She goes back and put the knife back up and goes in our room and slams the door. I take a quick ass shower, brush my teeth, spray on some Polo Black, and put on a brand-new pair of all black Polo boxer briefs. I walk into the room, step in the closet and select a pair of all white Ones, blue B.R. jeans and an all white B.R. collar shirt. I put my shit on as quick as possible and I hit the door.

I swing by the L store and grab a bottle of Remy Martin V and a pack of Newport shorts in the box and two boxes of Gold labels. I pull up at the Baptist car wash and get old school Hollywood to clean my car and shine my rims up for me.

I was the only car here at first. Now, this bitch is looking like Crenshaw. Niggas and bitches is everywhere, loud music is playing from at least five cars, and the cush is in the air.

I got the same ole crew; Playboy, Ron, Roddy, Lil Charles, Black and a few more niggas. We be on some real ass playa shit and we ain't looking for no bullshit, but we ain't ducking no wrecks either and we gone get at cha bitch so you better keep her ass close if you trying not to get played.

We been parking lot pimping for a few hours and the night is still young, so we decide to swing down Asher and see what the town is looking like. I'm in the old school black on chrome, Playboy in the all candy blue Tahoe with the candy blue 26s, Roddy in the Durango, Lil Charles in the DTS and it's candy on chrome. Ron in the blue and gray 300 and we in one line and pulling up. This is just how it goes down in the Roc town on the weekends.

Kum n' Go is off the chain, but the timers are always over there, so we push past that bitch, but Kroger's parking lot is going off as well, so we pull in and hop out over there.

The younger crowd is doing donuts and smoking out the Dollar Tree parking lot, and people are just constantly riding through. About 12:45, we head in the direction of the Hill.

You know we gots to park VIP. Real niggas don't park they shit down the hill. You might come out and your shit could be gone, or some hating ass nigga or bitch done threw a brick through your window or something. So, I pay $25 for VIP parking.

We park and fall in the club and it's jumping. As we walk in I hear DJ Deja Blu say, "Hear come them 23rd Street boys," and even though I've been home for over two or three months now, he still says, "Welcome home to Truth, AKA Bighood Tha Don."

I nod my head in his direction and we keep right on pushing to the bar in the back of the club where my homeboy Roddy baby momma is the bartender. I slide her a hundred and she gives me a stack of brown paper towels. In the middle of the stack is my very small nine-shot shot .22 cal.

Ever since Dink got killed in the club, I don't go to none of the others unless I find myself someone to give a C-note to slip my shit in and wait for me to come. If I don't come, just take it back home with you and I still will find time to bring $100 to you at your house or wherever. Before I leave, every time, I make sure to give it back to her, because this is my club strap only.

I slide it into my pocket and then I give her another $100 and tell her to keep the drinks coming. Me and Playboy shoot a few games of pool, and then in comes Trice and her crew, but it's like 2:45, and she is already toasted. Her home girls are mad cause she made them bring her here to meet me, so once they spot me, they dump her drunk ass off on me and bounce!

I tell my guys that it's a night for me. I slide back to the bar, tell fam to keep the drinks going to my table as long as she sees Playboy, and I slide her the deuce deuce back. I snatch Trice's ass up and head straight to the hotel where I fuck her motherfucking brains out, from about 3:00 till about 8:00 in the AM. Then I finally fall asleep.

I wake up right before checkout time. I grab my phone off the night table and see that I have at least forty missed calls from my baby momma. I know she is pissed the fuck off, so I wake Trice up, take a quick shower with her and take her to her car, which is at her homegirls' house.

I then head home thinking of a lie to tell so I won't have to go through the bullshit.

V. P. Taylor

# (Truth) Life Goes On

I'm driving on the freeway headed home and I call my baby momma to tell her that I went out last night and that I had too many drinks and that I didn't trust myself enough to drive home, so I slept on Black's couch. She didn't believe me for shit, but she lets it go for the moment. But trust me, I know that this shit is not over.

It takes me about fifteen minutes to get to the house from Little Rock, give or take a few minutes, for traffic. I-630 is a motherfucker, believe me. As I pull into the carport, the side door flies open and out comes my baby momma looking at me all crazy and shit.

She says, "You smell like cheap motel soap. Who was the bitch, Tyreque, huh? Who was she? Why you can't be a man and just tell me the truth, huh Tyreque?"

I'm like, "Dude, I have a headache and no time for this bullshit. Now baby, I have told you where I was and why I was there. Now can we please go inside?"

"No nigga, you go inside, I'm going over my homegirl house and get drunk, and while I'm at it I might just slip and fall on her little brother's dick!"

Now it's my turn to play mad because if I don't, that's just a whole 'nother bag of bullshit that I will have to deal with.

So, I just say, "Dude, you ain't going nowhere but in that kitchen to cook me something to eat. Now go on. I done told you that I got a headache from all the Remy V I drank. Now please baby can we leave this shit alone?"

And with that she just storms into the house and starts acting like she's putting on clothes to leave. So, I have to stop her. I reach and grab her and just fall back onto our bed and just hold her while she pretends that she wants to be let up. We both know that all she wants is my attention.

After about 10 minutes of playing around she asks what do I want to eat and I tell her whatever you feel like cooking, and I let her up. She gets up and goes into the kitchen and washes up and starts to putting some food together. While she's doing her thing, I turn on my Xbox One and start to play 2k12, when my phone rings.

I look at the screen and see that it's Lou. I answer, "What up, old man?"

He answers, "Nothing much, youngster. I need you to come by the shop later and meet my nephew. How's eight o clock sound?"

I tell him, "That's fine, G. I'm at the house about to eat, and when I get ready to move and groove shortly, I'll see you there."

I pick my joystick back up and start back playing 2k12. I'm wondering why Lou wants me to meet with his nephew, and why so soon?

My baby momma calls from the kitchen and says my food is ready: fried chicken, mac 'n cheese, green beans, and red cool aid.

While I'm eating, she comes and tells me that she is about to go to her grandmother's house to pick up the kids and asks if I be here when they get back. I tell her yeah, but I know that I may leave right behind her, 'cause if I'm going to see Lou, I may as well take him some money, so I need to check a few traps along the way. It's still early though, so I have a little time.

Once I'm done eating, I wash the dishes, make three plates for them, and put the rest up. I place their plates in the oven and grab my phone and my keys. On my way out I forget that I was going to write them a note, so I go back inside and jot down a fast little note apologizing to the kids for not being there when they got home. I tell my baby momma that if she's a good girl, she might get her back blowed out when I get back home.

This time I leave the old school and jump in to my 2011 Tahoe, also black with black leather interior and some 24"rims. I'm riding high and on my way to the hood to pick up some money from a few of the homies, so when I see Lou tonight, I can clear up my last tab and get shit back crackin' with a fresh new batch.

This corn is really selling like a muthafucca, but it's really not my game. I've been planning on telling Lou that we need to get with some faster shit, but him being from the old school and all, I just can't see him doing it, so I've been holding my thoughts to my chest, feel me?

I pull out my phone and call Mannie, and as soon as he picks up he is like, "I'm ready OG, meet me at my sis house in 10 minutes."

I tell him, "Bet," and hang up.

My next call is to my nigga C Boy and he tells me that he's ready as well. So, shit it's like 5:45, so I got like two and a half hours to play with. I pull up at CRIP 6 and see my nigga Low Down coming out the store.

He's like, "Truth what it do, Cuzzo?"

"Ain't shit my nigga what up with you?"

"Finna go to the park and fire up a stick. You with it?"

"Naw loc, I'm straight on that. I ain't hit no stick since the '90s."

He says, "Well drop me off then."

I say, "Ok. Let me get some Newports right fast."

When I walk into the 6 the Arab behind the glass says, "OG, what's up with you today?"

"Not shit Moe, how bout you?"

"Oh, same shit every day. What you need, a pack of Newport shorts in the box?"

"You know it. That's why I pass up every store in the hood to come fuck with you."

--------

Low Down is standing by my ride when I come out and I tell him to come on, big homie, let's ride. I drop him off and hit him with a few ends and head to Mannie's sister's house. When I pull up, I see cuz outside about to get into it with some lil nigga. I hop out like, "What's going on out here?"

Mannie's sis is like, "This hoe ass nigga keep putting his hands on me and I done had enough."

While she's telling me all this some more niggas is pulling up and hoping out, so I grab the strap from the stash.

I say, "Hold up, it ain't going down like this." I tell the lil playa, "You got a problem putting your hands on the lady and her brother ain't leaving, so you call your homies and they down with you and all, but I know ain't no nigga ready to die about this shit. You and her will most likely be back together after I kill all these niggas, so just tell them to get back into the car and bounce and stop putting your hands on my nigga sister. That way all of us can keep getting money and keep on pushing, you feel me?"

The lil nigga looked at the FN 57 in my hand and said, "Truth, you right my dude," then he turns and tells Mannie and his sister, "Look OG Mannie, I apologize," and then he says to Tonya, "Baby, I'm sorry you know I wasn't trying to hurt you."

She just looks at him and says, "Whatever nigga. Next time I'm a shoot your ass."

Soon the crowd clears and Mannie walks over to his car and grabs a Gucci bag out of the back seat. He walks back over and tosses it into my back seat, and then he tells me it's all there.

He laughs and says, "Who the hell you think you are with all this smooth ass talking and shit?"

Now it's my turn to laugh and I say, "The nigga that had your back and didn't even have to aim my shit at a nigga!"

All Cuzzo could say was, "True. True. When you gone get at me with that other?"

I just tell him make sure he answers the phone when I call, and he walks off and heads for his sister's house. With that I'm headed to holla at C-boy.

I call his phone and he tells me that he is at the Days Inn on Fair Park in room 245 in the back. "Ok Crip, I'll call when I pull in. Give me about 10 minutes. I'm hopping on the freeway at Woodrow."

When I pull up, I see bro walking down the steps with a big bag on his arm. I'm already thinking 'bout putting all of the money into that backpack and Mannie ain't gone see the Gucci no more.

He jumps in like, "What up, OG?"

"Not shit my nigga. Pick up when I call you. I got you homie."

He says, "Ok my nigga," and he hops out. I pull off.

My moms lives right down the street, so I head that way. It's like 6:45, and I need to count this money so I can see if I need to put something with it or not. I hate not having everything in its proper place. If I say $100,000 Monday then it's gone be $100,000 Monday. Never be late and never be short, always keep your word, and always understand that business is business and that business is never personal.

I grab both bags from the back seat and put them next to me in the front seat. I'm pulling up on the side of my mom's house where I can count the Gucci bag, $40,000 and then the bigger one $60,000 and it's only Sunday! I love it when shit works out perfectly!

I put all of the money into the bigger bag and push it on the floor in the front seat and toss the Gucci in back, then I climb out and lock the doors. I walk into my mom's house and say, "Momma what's up?"

"Aww nothing baby," she says, "just glad your home and looking out for them grandsons of mine! That baby boy reminds me so much of you till it's scary."

I promise her that he will be ok and then I kiss her and tell her that I have a meeting at 8:00 tonight, and I'm out the door, into my truck and headed for West Little Rock to meet with Lou and his nephew.

V. P. Taylor

# (Truth) Mo Money, Mo Problems

When I pull into the parking lot it's 7:55. I park and head into the shop. As always, there's no one else there besides Lou and his nephew.

Lou stands and says, "Tyreque, it's good to see you. This is Ricky my nephew. Ricky, this is Tyreque. He and Dinky were like brothers. Dinky told me all about Tyreque when he was in federal prison and since he's been home, he has gone through a lot, but every word that I was told about him has been true indeed. He is loyal, and trustworthy, and will kill at the drop of a hat. Speaks his mind yet is very respectful. Ricky, I am telling you all of this 'cause I loved Dinky like a son. You know that. Dinky loved Tyreque so much that he would not work with me if I didn't give him my word that when Tyreque came home, I would at least meet with him. Unfortunately, he was killed, but as a man of my word, I told Lucky to bring him to me the minute he was ready to make someone pay for the death of my son, and his brother. Once I laid eyes on him, I knew why Dinky made such a request. Now I am telling you that my nephew, you too can trust him."

The whole time that Lou was talking, me and Ricky was looking at one another. Lou looked at me and said, "My son, see me before you leave," and with that, he turned and left the room.

Ricky said, "I have never heard my uncle speak of anyone as highly as he just did you. I am impressed as well. and honored to meet you. I would like to discuss a discreet matter with you. Are you interested?"

I tell him yes, I'd be glad to help him, if indeed I may.

Ricky explains to me that he has been in business with a few people for a few years and all of a sudden when he drops on them something nice and heavy, they seem to feel like they don't have to pay any more. Seems that as long as he was hitting the lil dude off with a pound or two of ice and 3 or 4 pounds of cush, he would make the dough and come back. Well, since he got 10 pounds of ice and 10 pounds of cush, Ricky has not heard from him, and he will not answer the phones.

"So, what would you like me to do?" I ask.

He said that he wants to give me double that to kill the dude, and he would love it if I would work with him, since his last partner is no longer able to. He will start off with giving me 20 pounds of ice and 20 pounds of cush, same price as his last dude for the first six months, then $1000 less each six months, but each six months my supply doubles. It's really an offer I would be stupid to turn down.

First, he was giving the little dude ten pounds of ice at $4,000 a pound so that's $40,000, plus ten pounds of cush at $3,000 per pound, which is $30,000, to sleep the lil dude! Then he's gonna front me twenty and twenty, and the same four points and four points for the first six months then go to four points and two points, but then the next six months, it goes to forty and forty. Once I get done thinking shit out, I tell him that he has a deal. We shake on it, and he gives me all the info that I'll need to get things moving.

--------

Ricky thanks Lou for the introduction and tells him that I'll be right back. I then run to my truck and get my book bag with his cash inside. Lou smiles and says that this is what Dinky wanted, and that he is not surprised that things are working out so well. He tells me to get two new 57's so he can change the lands and grooves in the old ones. I ask why, and he gave me three very good reasons.

With brand new 57s in hand and a mission to accomplish, I get straight to work. The first thing I do is type the nigga name in and let Facebook put a face to the name that I have.

I don't know why these youngsters these days don't understand that all the attention that they crave will and can get them killed! This lil dude is no exception. He is going live on Facebook talking about how he got money to blow and showing pounds of loud like he got a pass to do this shit! And then he makes the biggest mistake of all, the kind that can cost a nigga his life. He tells the world where he will be tonight, and then he flashes a new car, which shows what he will be driving as well!

So, being as though I don't want a gang of people seeing me tonight, I come up with a smooth ass game plan and I pray like hell that it works.

Little Rock is only so big, and all of the night spots are conveniently in the same general part of town. That makes my job easy. I met this lil black ass bitch through my main man Dinky. He was fucking the lil bitch, and when he died, she started coming at me.

I'm in her car tonight, but I took her tag off and got a dealer's plate that I stole off of another car and put on her shit! I'm just parked in lil spots here and there around town cause the night is getting old and the crowds are going to start coming through. Once I spot my man's car, the games will begin.

At this point I'm sitting in the parking lot beside Kum N' Go on Asher. I've been sitting here for about forty minutes when I see a rush of cars pulling in. The third car is the one that I'm looking for. I sit up and look at the picture on my phone and then look back at the dude that gets out of the new red charger with the temp tags on it. It's my guy, and now the clock starts.

To my surprise he is riding solo. He's parked by one of the gas pumps, so I pull just a lil bit closer to see if I can overhear anything. There's about twelve people all together, just parked and standing outside of their cars talking, when I hear him tell his man, "Y'all wait for me right here, I got to run across the street and pick up this bitch for the night."

Across the street is the Town and Country apartments. This is where he makes his last mistake, 'cause I can get his ass over there right in the parking lot. I cross the street ahead of him. It's one way in and the other way out. As soon as I pull in, I cut the lights and park as fast as I can. I'm sitting there when he pulls past me, and when I think he's about to go all the way to the back, he then parks illegally, hops out and runs in between the buildings.

This is my chance, so I get out and as he comes back through the middle, he steps between two cars and starts to take a piss. I walk up and say, "Nice car!"

He turns to get a look at me, and I shoot him in the chest. As he falls, I walk up and double tap him in the head and walk back to the car. I get inside, turn the lights on, drive the wrong way out, and head straight down Asher. I pull over in the cut by Goodfellas Barbershop and put the right tags back on and toss the other ones. Now I'm on my way to this lil bitch house to get my ride and a shot of head before I head home.

By the time I make it back to her house, I have changed my mind. I don't feel like fucking with her, as she has already served her purpose for the day. Now all I want is to get away from the lil bitch.

I hate messy bitches. They just seem to never respect the fact that they ain't shit but side bitches, and this bitch ain't even worth that title. She was just a piece of ass.

I give her the keys to her car and twenty dollars for gas. I tell her that I will see her later. She's upset 'cause I told her that I would spend the night with her, but I'm not feeling it, and what I really need right now is some Remy Martin V and a game plan, 'cause shit is about to get real!

Mo' money, mo' problems!

And with that thought, I hop into my ride and head straight for Pic Pac on 12th street. It's crazy how things seem to be moving so fast, and I'm a thinker, so I can't believe that this same time last year I was in the feds wishing I was where I am right now!

I'm telling myself to be careful 'cause this shit is real life and death games that I'm out here playing!

The parking lot is packed, and I see a few niggas that I know, so I get out and tell one of them to look after my ride while I run in the store. I leave it running 'cause this is Blood hood, and just because I grew up around here and my family is still over here don't mean that I can just be careless of what can happen. Shit I've only been out five months and I got four bodies already: three personal, and one business.

I got my drink, and thank my dudes for watching my ride, and toss them both a five-dollar bill. I jump behind that tint and start to fix my drink. I like my shit 'straight-no-chaser' with four ice cubes.

My phone rings and it's my homeboy Ron.

"What up, loc?"

He says, "Not shit, Cuzzo, what you got going on?"

"Pulling away from Pic Pac, why?"

Ron said, "Slide by here before you get too far away."

"Ok Crip. Give me about 5 minutes."

Cuzz lives right around the corner, maybe six or seven blocks from the liquor store. I head that way. The whole time I'm thinking about all this dope I'm going to have to get rid of.

When I pull up, bro is outside playing with his pit bull and smoking a blunt.

I say, "What up bro?"

Ron says, "Where you headed?"

"Nowhere, just left from off Asher trying to see what the town is looking like."

He says, "They say some lil nigga just got slumped across from Kum N' Go!"

"At them apartments?" I ask.

Ron confirms, "Word, bro. You know how these young niggas is. Shit, they kill for breakfast!"

Avoiding the topic of conversation, I say, "Let me make a quick call real fast."

I jump back into my ride and call Ricky phone. When he picks up and says hello, I just tell him I'm looking forward to having a great year, and that I really appreciate the opportunity that he and his family are giving me. I tell him he has my number and I hang up!

I get back out the ride and tell Ron that we are about to turn the fuck up around this bitch!

He asks, "What you got in mind, big homie?"

I tell him that I'm about to hit him with that gas for the low low, but I can't take no loss at all. I tell him just answer the phone when I call.

I drive away from Cuzzo house doing the math in my head. I'm thinking the first few times I'm dumping slabs for $3,600 and zips for $250. At $250 a zip, I will make $4,000 off each slab and slabs at $3,600 that's $36,000 for the whole ten, so that's $6,000 for me from the gas, and then the ice my number is $4,000. I'm dumping them at $10,000, so I'll be dropping Ricky $70,000 and my take home is $66,000.

After thinking about money and all that shit, I have had a change of heart. I've been out of prison five months and shit just ain't the same no more. My nigga Dinky gone and my so-called hood is really a joke.

I been out making moves and taking chances, and I don't give a damn about shit but staying out of prison and getting some motherfucking money. I don't know if it's the Remy that I've been drinking or what, but right now I'm feeling myself and I'm out, making money, and smashing niggas solo dolo, and can't shit stand in my way!

I pull up by Cin Park and just thumb through my contacts and Facebook. Hoes been chasing me since I got out, but I been too busy trying to get shit in proper perspective. I really have not been thinking about no pussy! But that's what's on my mind right now, so I call Playboy up and see what he got popping for tonight.

We can fall up in the 50/50, have a few drinks, and see what strippers we can go knock off. But bro says he got his lil ones, and it'll be late as hell when he can get out. So, I'm like cool, ain't no problem, I'm solo dolo, and more for me.

While I'm sitting on the hood, my homeboy Cory Crip Cuzz pulls up in his lil gray van and tells me he needs to get a half of thang. I tell him I don't have it on me, and that he can go by my mom's crib and my lil nephew will hook him up.

My nephew is one rock selling motherfucker. I mean cuzz be having shit jumping like the '90s. Gotta give homie his due, cause boy that game there for most niggas been fatal!

He tells me to call him and make sure nephew is in place.

I do, he is.

He heads that way.

So, I'm back to Facebook and Instagram and my shit don't be playing. My DMs stay full and I got like, ten messages on FBM, all females, but none that I want to entertain.

I mean I know I can call Trice, Mercedes, or Diamond, but I know don't none of these hoes really give a fuck about me, and I'm really tired of blessing motherfuckers with my time that don't deserve it!

## (Truth) Building An Empire

While sitting there playing with my phone, it rings and it's Ricky's number. I answer.

"Hello, Truth my man. What are you up to?"

"Not much," I answer. "Just sitting in my neighborhood trying to find something to get into, if you know what I mean?"

"Yeah, I know what you mean, and I may be able to help you out with a few of your problems," he says.

"Oh yeah and how can you do that my brother?"

"Just write this address down and come see for yourself."

The address was 10018 Lucy Lane. I punched it into my GPS and was on my way. By the time I got there it was about 10:45 at night, and I was ready to talk business! I pulled out my phone and texted Ricky and told him I was outside.

After a few seconds, a bad ass Mexican girl opened the door and came to my window. She looked at me for a moment or two and then said, "Let's go inside, Papi."

The house was a two-story brick house. It was the type of house that I wished I could have grown up in.

The inside was decked out in black leather and gray carpet throughout. Every room that I could see into was draped all in black and gray!

As I followed her through the house and down to the basement, I could not help but watch her ass sway from side to side in them tight ass stretch pants she was wearing. Them shits looked painted on. The bitch was bad, and she knew it! As we were coming up on the door, she stopped and turned to me.

"This is as far as I can go," she told me. "There's a little black button on the far wall. If you need anything, just press it and someone will come."

I ask, "Are you going to be that someone?"

She says, "Maybe. Now, excuse me. I have to go, and don't be looking at my ass!"

All I could do was smile and watch as she moved back the way we had come. The door opened and there was Ricky smiling at me. He looked past me to see what I was looking at and said, "Come in. She's beautiful, huh?"

"Who is she?"

He just looked at me with a slight smile and said, "Later. Let me show you what we're working with."

The room is just as all the others - decked out in black leather - but in this one, the floor is black as well. Ricky grabs a black bag from behind the couch and hands it to me. I look inside and find stacks of rubber banded blocks of money neatly placed in the bag. $140,000 in cash. Then he grabs ten pounds of weed and ten pounds of ice and places them into two bags and says, "Make sure that your things are properly placed before we continue our night!"

But me, I'm thinking, *why don't I just pay for this shit right now, that way I'm not working for him but with him.*

So, I say, "Ricky, if it's ok with you I'd like to pay for this now and kill the debt process."

Ricky smiled at me and said, "I knew you was a real businessman. Now you are in business for yourself. I was prepared to go either way. Had you chosen the other way, it would have only showed that you are not ready to be a boss of a whole neighborhood. My uncle knew that you were ready. I was just waiting to see."

I smile and tell him thanks, and then I sit the bag of money down and count out $70,000. I drop it into one of my other bags and hand him the bag with the other $70,000 in it. I then walk over to the door and press the button on the far wall. When the beautiful lady appears, I inform her that I need to go to my car. She turns and leads the way. This time her ass is not even a thought.

Money is on my mind and I'm building an empire!

Once I make it to my car, I place the two bags in the back on the floor and re-lock the doors. I turn and ask, "What's your name?"

She has a beautiful smile, and says, "Maria."

"Maria, can we see each other again?"

"Maybe. I'll let you know. Are you going back inside?"

"I don't know. Should I?"

Maria says if I ever want to see her again that I better not! She tells me that Ricky is going to have a party, and it's going to be a lot of nasty shit going on. She explains that if I am a part of it, then no, I will not see her again.

I smile and say, "Tell Ricky that I'll call him later."

She asks to see my phone and dials her number from my phone then hands it back with a smile. She walks back up the stairs to the house, ass swaying from side to side, and again I am looking. She stops, turns and looks at me and winks an eye. She mouths the words 'I'll call you.'

Maria leaves me standing there with a stupid ass smile on my face and a hard ass dick.

I get into my ride and head home. I'm calling all my niggas and letting them know that I got the zips of gas for $250 and the slabs for $3,600. I call my homeboy Mack and tell him the number on the skates. He says he'll make some calls and get back with me.

Once I get home I head straight to the carport where the old school is parked. I put the work into the trunk and take the money into the house with me. I have one of those little Walmart safes that cost like $130. I put the bag in there. It'll have to do till I need a bigger one, feel me?

--------

My baby momma is on the bed, still somewhat mad about how shit been going since I came home. I mean, shit. I didn't plan for shit to turn out this way. My home boy getting killed, like that fucked me up and really pushed me right back into that way of life. It's kill or be killed out here, and me personally, if I'm playing the game, then best believe I'm playing to win at any cost.

I kick off my shoes and clothes and get into the bed next to her and say, "Hey baby how as your day?"

She says, "Fine Tyreque. Where have you been all day? Laid up with one of your lil new hoes?"

"No, I have not been laid up with no hoes, I've been out handling my business."

She says, "Good, cause both your car notes are coming up and I need my hair and nails done!"

I just roll my eyes and get out of bed and go into the safe and count out $2500 and toss it on the bed next to her. I go into the living room and turn on my Xbox One. No thank you or none of that shit, and our car notes together probably ain't shit but like $1500 anyway. I play 2k12 until I fall asleep.

When I wake up the next morning, the house is empty, and I'm still on the couch in the living room, only someone took the liberty to toss a blanket over me. I get up and head to the bathroom to take a piss, wash my hands, brush my teeth and wash my face. The bedroom is clean and there's a note on the bedside table.

> *Took the kids to school, won't be back*
> *until after one o'clock. The word for the*
> *day is JOB.*

I smile at the note and toss that bad boy right into the trash can. I'm thinking, *I got a job alright, and I'm the shift supervisor, the manager and the C.E.O.*

With that thought I'm headed to the carport to get the bags and get them into the kitchen so I can get shit ready for the streets!

I call Mack and ask if he has heard anything about the skates. He tells me yeah, but they want to see how good the shit is first. I tell him that I'll bring him a half a thang at four stacks, but that I don't want to meet them. He can get whatever they want from me and take it to them.

I know how shit can go south real fast in this game. Ain't no love and these young niggas don't respect shit no more. All they want to do is rob and steal, when they really some cowards on the cool. A nigga will kill you for fucking his girlfriend but talk shit about you for taking $50,000 from him! I can hear the shit now, "Oh that lil fifty wasn't nothing. I fuck that off in the strip club." Let him find out you fucked his girl,? "I'mma kill that hoe ass nigga for that disrespectful ass shit"

Naw, I don't want to meet no motherfuckers.

I tell Mack that I'll meet him at Exxon on Markham. I hang up with him and call my nephew and tell him that I got that gas on deck and that he can holla at me or whatever, but that all shit gots to go through him, 'cause I don't want to meet no one!

I take out two pounds, one of each, a half pound of skates and eight zips, then sixteen zips of gas. I got all this shit in a Gucci backpack. I'm headed out the door when I think that it might be a good idea to strap myself. I go to my room, get my XD 40.cal with the dick out, put it into the bag with the work and set that shit by the back door. Then I go find something to wear.

My closet is big as fuck, and it's a walk in. It's shit in that bitch still with tags on it. Your boy don't bullshit when it comes to the threads. Gots to be clean at all times. I might not shave, but a nigga gone be fly at all times, even if I'm in a gas station T-shirt and 501s.

On this day I decide on 501 shorts, a T-shirt, a pair of blue and grey Air Malcolm Plus, and a blue LA Dodgers snap back. Outfit complete, I step out the room, grab my bag at the door and jump into my 2012 Camaro SS. I snatch the XD out the bag and toss it on the floorboard of the passenger seat, and head towards Exxon on Markham to meet Mack. I call him and tell him I'll be there in ten minutes.

Now that I've met my home boy and dropped off the half pound to him, I'm headed to the hood so I can start dumping this gas, and of course you know I got to slide by the barber shop and holla at Black.

--------

When I first walk in the shop, everyone that's in there stops talking. When they see that it's just me, they start right back at it. Black is probably the best barber in the whole damn city, if you ask me, and he keeps a busy shop. Most of the guys that get cut here are major players in the game, so I fit right in. I tell my dude what up, and I give a few handshakes here and there, then I sit down.

I got a few of them zips in my Gucci tote bag, and it's sitting across my lap. All of a sudden, everyone turns my way, and someone says, "Damn bro you smell good as fuck."

I'm slow cause this shit is all new to me, so I just say, "Thanks, ok good looking."

But these niggas is like blue tick hound dogs or some shit, cause they like, "Where's it at?"

Then it dawns on me that it's the cush that they smell. I'm thinking that Polo Black is the truth!

I say, "Oh yeah, that's what I came through for, to holla at the Big Homie and let him know that I got the gas on deck."

Black stops cutting the head he's on and says, "Truth, let me holla at you real fast." We walk in the back.

He's like, "What's the ticket?"

I tell him it's $250 a zip and $3,600 a pound, and since this is one of my day-one niggas from way back in the gap, I tell him that as long as the cash is right, ain't no limit on what I can get!

He gives me $500 on the spot and takes both the ones I came in with and said bring him fourteen more. I tell him I'll be right back and go back to the car and grab my bag.

After selling the first pound to my home boy, I'm on my way back to the house to get more when Mack calls and tells me that he done with that and he needs more. I ask him how much more, and he tells me his sister's boyfriend wants two, and his home boy wants three! As you can see, my day has just started and shit is going great!

If these few plays Mack has set up go smoothly, then I've made all my money back and still got plenty to work with.

I could get used to this shit. It's crazy how one minute shit can be all bad and the next all good! But that's the way of the world.

So, while I'm on the freeway headed home, these are the thoughts that are running through my mind: *I don't want to get the big head and start to make myself stand out, plus I know where I come from, and I damn sure know where I ain't trying to go back to!*

I'm trying to check myself; 'cause shit can go south fast in these Little Rock city streets.

I let the carport door up from the street, and as I'm pulling in, I make sure that it's all the way back down before I get out the car. I know all the little Jack Boy tricks and ain't none of them gone work with me. My hand is on the heat and ready to blast anything that move when I get out the car. I can't take no chances.

These thoughts is the proof that I'm all the way back into the game that I said I was done with!

I call Mack before I get this shit together, 'cause I don't want to make no unnecessary trips with all this work. He answers and tells me that everything is cool and gives me the room number. He tells me to come on so I can get there before anyone else.

That's what's up, so I'm headed to Motel 6 on Markham to sell two dudes five pounds of ice. I trust Mack with my life.

I'm not the least bit worried about being in this dump with over $50,000 cash on me, plus me and Mack are an odd pair, him being 6"1' and white, and me 5"9' and as black as the Ace of Spades, with dreads.

I get out the car and grab my backpack and make my way to the room. Mack opens the door looking like the FBI or something, and says, "Come in. Come in. Give me the work and go back to the car. They're here!"

So, I do as I'm told. Like I said, I trust this white boy with my life, and as I'm going to the car, I pass two white dudes and a white girl that's so damn fine I can't keep from looking at her. They go right into Mack's room and slam the door.

About 3 minutes goes by and then my phone rings and Mack is saying, "Bro, come here for a sec." So I grab the XD and head back to the room.

Bro knows these dudes, and they are trying to use that to get him to let them pay for four of them and get the last one on the front, but Bro was telling them that the shit is not his, so he can't do it, but he'll let them talk to me.

Now the first thing I'm thinking is that I didn't want to meet no one, but by this being his sister and her people I let it go. But I still tell them that I don't know them like that, and unless they got the money, no dice!

They had the money and the play was made. Once they leave, I give Mack his other half. I count the money accountant-fast, and I'm out the door.

Now I'm headed back to my house again for the second time today. I'm dropping off $57,000 and I keep the $600 for pocket change. As I'm pulling into my driveway, my phone goes off. I answer.

"Hey, I hope this is not a bad time for me to be calling you. I know you got a girl and everything, but I have been thinking about you and just had to call."

I have no clue who this is. I say, "No this is not a bad time, but who am I speaking with?"

A smile spreads on my face when the voice on the other end responds, "Maria!"

"Hello beautiful how are you? I didn't think you were going to call."

Maria said, "I told you I would. I'm true to my word, Mr. Truth. Always. So why do people call you Truth?"

"Well, for now let's just say because I'm true to my word as well!"

"Is that right?"

"Yes, it is!"

She says that that's good to know. We have at least one thing in common! She said she was glad that she called, and that she promises to call again.

I finally get out of the car and go straight to the safe, put the money inside, toss the bag into the living room and stop by the kitchen to grab a Bud Light out the fridge!

Now I've got nine pounds of gas and four pounds of ice left. I'm thinking that I have nothing else to do, so I call my homeboy Derrick, just to see what he's been up to.

# (Trinity) On The Block

I was around thirteen when gangs and violence were becoming an epidemic. I was beginning to lose friends to drive-by shootings and violence.

I had several friends who were full-fledged gang members. Drug dealers. My neighborhood, that used to be fairly safe, was now on Orange, high alert status.

There were two primary gangs: the Bloods and the Crips, with the Bloods being larger and having more territory, but the Crips being more solidified as a group. I lived on Oak Street, which was Bloods territory. Most of my friends were Bloods at school and at home.

I rarely saw many Crips. I had never really been interested in joining either gang. I had grown up in that neighborhood, so by the time I had made it to adolescence the boys in my neighborhood were of no interest to me.

My older brother was never involved in any of that type of stuff and I was never pressured to join. I always felt safe, partly because I wasn't gang affiliated, and I knew almost everyone in my neighborhood, and I minded my own business (remember Hood 101?).

I came and went as the average teen, but I was always cautious and aware of my surroundings. I learned to read people and situations and learned how to 'move around' if things look to be getting out of hand. I wasn't really fearful of much. I didn't have as clear an understanding of death and danger as I have now. When my friends would pass, I would grieve, but it was almost like it came with the territory. So many people, kids really, were being shot and killed back then that you really didn't have a lot of time to adjust. You just kept moving.

During my junior high days, I was involved in some of everything. I was on student council, peer facilitators, beta club, national junior honor society and so on. I had all advanced classes and did well in them for the most part. I did well in school but I was a little on the wild side. I was an adventurer and outgoing. I was also a fighter. I didn't mind fighting and would sometimes bully others to get my way.

Candace was that way as well. We stayed in low-grade trouble during junior high. Jewells was the opposite. I don't think she ever got into a fight with anyone other than her siblings. We were all smart and active in school.

And the boys? Let's just put it like this: we had our picks and chooses.

Candace and I were more on some player type stuff, I believe largely from the influence of having older brothers.

We saw how boys lied, played games and broke hearts and we were determined to not get played. Jewells was the good girl for a long time and had one boyfriend with whom she held hands (lol). I had always had male attention from the guys in the neighborhood and the boys at school. Hey, face it. Boys like girls. It's a law of nature.

I wasn't really serious about any of them. I had a few 'boyfriends' that I semi-committed to, but I liked boys more as friends back then. I'm like that to this day. You can't be my lover until you're my friend. I'll get bored with you as a lover, but a friendship never dies.

Our ritual usually was to go to the mall, go to the movies, go to the games, meet guys. It wasn't so much about having a lot of guys as much as it was variety. When you grow up in the same hood and attend the same schools, you just grow tired of each other. You had to venture out.

That's how I met him.

One of the benefits of being bused to different schools is that you get to meet different people. Branch out. I had grown really close with a friend from school who lived across town. I would often spend nights with her and she with me. We would hang out in her part of town more because there was less gang violence in that area.

I guess that's pretty much the only way I would have met a Crip. At the time I didn't know that he was one. I just knew I didn't know him and hadn't seen him around. I moved around a lot, but the skating rink, bowling allies, movies and malls were all Bloods occupied. In small towns, you tend to see the same people over and over again, so to meet someone that you've never seen before is a rarity.

It was then and there that I met him. A troubled soul, a bad boy, a Crip, and with whom, I would realize years later, would be my only experience of a soul binding relationship.

The courtship started slow. For one reason or another, I've subconsciously blocked out many of my memories of that time.

And trust me when I say I've blocked out that time. I know that many people don't remember things from their childhood, but I literally have an elephant's memory. I remember everything, which is probably why my head is so big.

No, seriously. I can vividly remember the way I felt in kindergarten at Garland Elementary School when I knew the answer to who conducted the Underground Railroad. I believe that was the creation of my nerdy 'thirst for information' side.

Because my memories have always been pretty vivid, I'm sure I *intentionally* blocked out some of my memories with him.

As a trained mental health professional, I am very aware of how people block out traumatic experiences, but I'm puzzled as to why I blocked out the awe inspiring, bubbly, butterfly in my stomach, lovey-dovey feelings for my first love. Well, twenty years later, they caught up with me. I'll talk more about that later.

What I have been able to conjure up in my memories, by pure willpower and cross-referencing with Jewells, Candace, my brother and 'him,' I can confidently write about it in some detail.

I was thirteen years old when I met him. Our birthdays are ten days apart. He's the eldest. I was at the $1 movie theater with my homegirl and he was with a friend.

He later told me he remembered what I wore that day — overalls. I don't remember, so he could have been embellishing the moment.

Anyway, it was a pretty standard 'boy sees girl, boy is attracted to girl, boy approaches girl, girl decides if she'll give him a shot,' which I did.

We exchanged numbers and began to 'talk' as we called it in those days.

I remember him being funny and sweet. I also remember him being a little shy at times, which came across, at times, as gamesmanship. He would quickly shift from being bold with me to getting really shy. I thought it was cute.

--------

At the time, I didn't know of his involvement in a gang. I certainly didn't know at what level he was involved. I don't know if that would have scared me away or not.

I remember we used to do things together. He wanted to be around and wasn't afraid to meet my family. He had done a few things with me and my family, such as movies, parades, etc.

I know we used to talk a lot, about what escapes my mind though. He used to do little silly teenage boy things when I was upset with him. He would beg me to forgive him, and I would play hard to get.

I've always had a no-nonsense type of personality, but those who really know me know that I am a softy.

I remember he would threaten to kill himself if I broke up with him, if I hung up the phone on him, etc. I never took him seriously and my little mean self would do things to call his bluff. Looking back, I'm so glad his little emotional self wasn't serious.

He was different from other boys and had a very soft and tender side to him, more so than I had seen with other guys. It was the thing back then to be 'hard.' He was the opposite, at least with me.

We talked on and off for a few months, and then for whatever reason, we stopped. Maybe he went on to greener pastures, or maybe I was so involved in school and my extra-curricular activities to be fazed, or maybe another guy caught my attention, who knows. He could have been locked up, I later realized.

I don't remember him from spring or summer that year. It's like he just disappeared out of my life and out of my psyche. I didn't think about him, didn't miss him. I moved on. That's what you do when you're young. You move on.

--------

In September of that same year, I got a call from him out of the blue. We literally just picked back up, full speed ahead. Like I said, initially we went really slow, talking daily and hanging out from time to time. This time was a blur. I blocked out the majority of our time together. It's like everything is in pieces.

*Did we kill someone back then? What the heck happened for us to be bound together like we were? I mean, seriously, what the freak happened?*

I had to rely a lot on my friends and on him to fill in the gaps. They told me that we were crazy in love, fun to be around, in love for real and that he would do anything for me, and I would do anything for him.

As a matter of fact, when I updated Jewells about our recent reconnection, she became nervous, even asking me where my husband and kids were, to assure herself that I hadn't run off with him. Everyone's responses scared me even more.

*If I shared a love so perfect, why did I black it out like that?*

I try to remember that time from September to May, but it's still fuzzy. I do remember we became sexually active fairly quickly during this time. I had lost my virginity over the summer to a guy that I was dating but didn't really care for. I was fourteen at the time and wanted to go ahead and get my first time out of the way. I didn't want it to be with someone I deeply cared for, because I didn't want to become "whipped." I know. Crazy, huh?

The average teenage girl wants to wait until that special someone comes along, but I was the opposite.

By the time he came back into my life, I felt ready.

I also remember our first time. I don't remember feeling anything magical. I just remember feeling like I wanted to please him. I was very inexperienced at the time and didn't know much about love or sex. I also wasn't one of those girls who loved the idea of love.

I loved the attention I got, not only from guys but also from being successful and popular in school. I wasn't worried about, love, relationships, white picket fences or happily ever-afters. I wanted to have fun, and he was a willing participant.

By this time, I had learned of his gang affiliation. It was kind of taboo at the time for me to date him. I wasn't affiliated with any gang, but as I stated earlier, the majority of my friends and family that were gang related were Bloods. I don't think I knew any Crips back then, at least not really well. They were more of the social pariahs then, and were smaller in number, and disliked by a lot of people.

It was all new to me, and I was open to different types of experiences and people. I think I've always been that way, which can be good and bad at times. I tend to accept people as they are. It doesn't matter. If I like you, I like you, and I'll fool with you. I don't care about what you do or what you've done.

Back then, I just liked him regardless of who or what he was. Eventually that like turned to love, and well, if you've ever been in love, you know how that goes.

# (Truth) Game Changer

Derrick's at his house, down the street from me. He asks if I'd take him to pay his phone bill. Me, with shit else to do, I tell him yeah.

When I pull up he is already outside. He jumps in and we pull off. I ask him where we we're going, and he says to the Sprint store on Shackleford. We head that way, talking shit the whole ride there, and laughing at each other about shit from the old days.

He gets out and goes in while I park and wait for him to handle his business. When he comes out, he says, "Guess who I just saw going into the store over there?"

"Who?"

"Your girlfriend Trinity."

Just the mention of that name sends all kinds of powers through my body. I mean, I have been through hell and back more than a few times in my life, and have faced all kinds of shit, but at that moment I didn't know what I felt, and this nigga's talking about come on let's go in!

I'm like, "No, hell no, you go!"

He says, "Are you scared or something?"

I was scared, because this person has been a constant thought in my head and in my heart for sixteen years or better, and yet I couldn't have told you if she was even alive until this very moment!

While I was in prison, I would lie in my bed and think about this girl that I was so madly in love with. I would wonder how my life might have been if Trinity and I had never broken up.

*Would she even know who I was if she saw me right now?*

All kinds of thoughts were going through my head. I have not seen her in at least seventeen years, and now I got this nigga trynna pull me out of my ride to go see her.

Finally, I get out and walk into the store with him, and he walks his ass right up to the table and says, "Hey Trinity."

When she looked up and I looked into her eyes, I felt something in my whole body. But I did not let on. At that moment all I could do was say, "Hello Trinity," and "it's wonderful to see you after all these years."

And we moved on.

But I can't explain to you the flood of emotions that my poor lil self felt at that time. I knew almost instantly that I was still madly in love with this woman!

When me and my home boy leave, I play like I'm cool and not tripping about who we just saw, but on the inside I'm fucked up, and I know the rest of my day is going to be as well.

I drop Derrick off and I'm just riding around with nowhere to go. My thoughts are consumed with her face, her eyes, her lips, her smell, and I know that I have to see her again. I have to talk to her. I have to say something, do something. I need her, I want her, and I will never ever let go.

-------

Running into Trinity last week like that has added yet another level to my game plan, and because of it, I'm second guessing everything that I am doing. I mean, I get it, I'm a hood nigga, I'm from the hood, but most niggas from the hood still haven't been through the things that I have gone through. Hell, just being my brother's little brother growing up was enough! But I made it through, and I built my own name and got myself sent to federal prison for it, and for or a long ass time, too.

I'd like to think that not many of my so-called friends would be able to stand up under that kind of pressure. Hell, I was getting jumped on by grown ass niggas when I was only twelve years old. Just because of who my brother was!

I'm twelve years old walking down the street one day, and a car pulls beside me and a dude asks, "Hey lil man you need a ride?"

I'm like, "No, I'm ok. My house is just right there." I point at a house right down the block. Well, they knew that I was lying, 'cause I was in their hood.

Another one looks up from the back seat and says, "Ain't you Lee's lil brother?"

I'm like, "Yeah." And niggas just started hopping out of all the doors. I was boxed in before I could even think of the word 'run'.

Now remember, I'm only twelve, but these fools are at least 15 or 16 years old, and shit, one of the niggas had to have been at least 18. They were punching, kicking and stomping me the hell out. Then one of them spit on me right before they jumped back into the car and pulled off.

This was an everyday thing, not just once or twice a week.

Shit. I had to watch where I went 'cause if I got spotted in the wrong hood, I had an ass whipping coming. And this is just a small part of the shit that I had to go through as a kid.

I just wanted to play ball and shit. But hell, I got tired of niggas jumping on me and shit, so instead of a basketball I carried a .22. And if I had to use it somebody was gone get shot.

These are just some of the things going through my head after I saw Trin.

I'm asking myself, *what are you doing? You're already back into selling drugs and shooting guns and shit like you done forgot that you just did all that time in prison.*

It's kind of like when Dink bka Dinky got killed. It sent me full speed ahead back into the streets! The switch was turned on.

But then seeing Trinity turned that bitch right back off. But of course, we know that the latter is never that easy! I always believed that a man doesn't reach his full potential until there's someone in this world that he loves more than he loves himself.

It's crazy that just seeing a person that you love can make you think so deeply, but it happened to me. I love this woman and I have not seen or spoken to her in over seventeen years.

*I don't know how she feels about me, and I don't even know if I'll ever see her again,* I'm telling myself, trying to get back into 'Truth' mode. *If I do see her again, I'll know that it is a sign, and I will at least tell her how I feel and get all of this shit off my chest.*

But right now, I've got business to handle, and I can't get shit done looking all googly- eyed and shit. But I cannot get this woman out of my head and I really don't want to. This is further evidence that I have it bad.

Doing all this thinking has me in a zone, and before I know it, I am almost to Conway. I was on the freeway just driving and thinking and was so consumed with thoughts of her and the shape of my life that, at that time, nothing else mattered.

# (Truth) Back to Business

I knew just the person to call to help me get back into that G mode that I needed to be in, and that's Lucky.

It's been a few months since we kicked it and I needed to be in the company of a real gangsta right now, 'cause this woman has got my head twisted like a motherfucker.

I call Lucky, but he's busy and can't talk at the moment. He must be on one or doing his thing, so that was out. At this point, I'm still just riding around, when Ricky calls and tells me that he has to go out of town for a few weeks.

He asks if I'm ok.

"Yeah," I tell him, "But I might really need you." Then I change that shit up quick even though it ain't like my shit ain't just flying off the shelf. "Is there someone I can contact if I need you?"

"Yeah, just call Maria and she will know what to do. I'll leave her twenty and twenty and tell her don't touch them unless you call."

I tell him thanks and we hang up.

Now I'm getting off I-630 at the Shackleford exit. There's a Denny's on my left. I pull into the parking lot and get out and just lean up against my car. For the life of me, I cannot shake the thoughts of seeing her again, but as much as I love and miss her, I just can't sit here looking like a lovesick puppy. I got all kinds of business to handle!

I make myself get back into the car and head home.

---------

For some reason, I'm thinking about shit that I was not thinking about before. Like it's not such a good idea to be keeping the work at the house! Hell, I should have thought about that shit from the jump.

*What if my P.O wants to come by or what if some lil nigga want to try to hit them a lick?*

Never keep shit where you lay your head!

I've been thinking about getting another car. The only reason I haven't was 'cause I didn't have the space. I'm thinking about renting a storage unit and putting the old school in it, and just leave the work in it. That way I can kill two birds with one stone.

I call ahead to see if Tasha, my baby momma, was at home. She picks up, but she is at Walmart, but can be there in 10 minutes. I tell her OK and to hurry up, 'cause I need her to follow me to a storage unit so I can put the old school in it. Then I tell her to go ahead and make some calls and find a good one.

I pull up to the house before she does. I get out of the car and go inside to open the door to the carport. I put all of the

work in one bag, minus two pounds of gas and one of skates.
I put them into the bag in the back seat of the Camaro.

When she pulls up, I go out to the truck before she gets
out and ask her, "Baby did you find anything?"

"Yeah, do you want to go to Little Rock or do you want
to stay out here in Maumelle?"

"Let's stay out here."

"Well, I hope something is taking its place, 'cause I'm tired
of driving this big ass truck, and that car you're in is too small
for me and the kids."

I'm like, "Ok. Ok. I'll get another car."

She pulls into the parking lot and we both get out and go
in together. She continues with the speech about how I have
too many cars and we need the room, 'cause she wants to get
a family car. So, she decided that we would put the old school
in storage.

I'm thinking, *why do the rental people have to know so much? Just
rent us the damn thing.*

Anyway, I tell baby that I only want it for 90 days and we
will pay for it up front. I buy a lock from them with two keys
and I keep them both. We pull on in to the unit. As I back
the old school in, I'm thinking that maybe I should rent a lil
house and keep the old school there. Well, for now I got 90
days to think about it.

--------

As soon as we pulled back up at the house, I jumped out the truck and headed straight into the house. I go into the bedroom into the closet and open the safe and do a quick count of my stash. I know there should be at least $127,000 in it. I had $70 left from the money that I got from Ricky, and I put $57 in there from my day-to-day trapping, minus the $2,500.00 I gave my baby momma.

The count is clear, so I close the safe back up and get ready to hit the streets.

------

It's 'bout time we get this shit back jumping round here! As I'm swinging through my old hood, I run across Fancy. She looking at the SS and says, "Damn nigga you came home shitting on these niggas, didn't you?"

Personally, I'm more of a laid-back type of dude, so I don't see it like that!

"Nah cuzz, it ain't like that, but peep this though. I need someone to rent a few spots for me around here. I'm trying to turn this bitch back up, you feel me?"

"What you got?" She asks.

"Nothing major. Just a lil gas, plus, you know I live out there in the subs, so I want to get the old school and the SS and bring them back on this side."

"Yeah, I feel you. When you trying to do this?"

"Like, yesterday, 'cause time is money, you dig?"

She takes my number and says that she on it and will call me in a few. In the meantime, I know that I must watch my step on this side of town, and you know that's a damn shame when you got to be careful in your own hood. But that's how it is these days. These niggas ain't shit but some real cutthroats who can't seem to get they ass in line. And 'cause of it they can't stand to see the next nigga eat.

Homies killing each other, plotting on they own 'cause they hustle ain't strong! And just because I came home on my own shit and trying to do half-ass good, I got to be trying to shit on a nigga. Nah, playa. I just ain't gone to be no damn Neanderthal and will not be left behind. And I ain't gone ask no nigga for shit. I'm a hustling ass playa paper chaser and that's just the way it is.

I never gave a fuck about the hood fame that I was given, but other niggas wanted it bad. Like right now, I don't feel like no OG or none of that shit, but other niggas be telling me, "Truth, what's wrong with you? You can't be walking around like that!"

And I'm like, "Why? Because of who you are. What you talking 'bout?"

They tell me, "Man you the face of 23rd Street. bro. It wasn't even cool to be a Crip until you came back home!"

But that ain't how I look at myself.

Other niggas in the hood that feel as though they should be in them shoes still hate me because whether I want it or not, I'm still looked at as an OG, and they don't like me because of it.

My brother always used to tell me, "Bro be careful, niggas like to see us against each other and if you ever let them catch you on your ass they will try to make you look bad!"

Me personally, I'm like fuck these niggas, and as long as they stay in they lane shit will be good! Cause I swear a nigga don't want these troubles that THE TRUTH is gone bring and that's a promise! So, the lil cats can stay in they lane and need to know that just 'cause you getting a lil money doesn't mean you no motherfucking OG.

Niggas laying around with army guns, robbing your ass blind right up under you, and ain't shit got shot, but nigga talking about what they gone do to Truth! One of the niggas up under you hit a lick on your dumb ass for two hundred pounds and made it look like Truth did it. Good luck, 'cause I don't play the losing game my nigga, and I ain't never had shit to say to the police.

While niggas was worried about me, they should have known better than to be talking on the stupid ass phones in the county jail. They got what's left of their family fucked off because they're too stupid to know to just shut the fuck up. And your lil pound puppy ass crew. Let's see how many of them gone stand beside you when them feds start to apply that pressure.

If you ask me, I think some of them is weak and will fold under questioning. I, however, keep it gangsta, and ain't no dirt on my name. I ain't never did shit but went hard for the hood! While niggas was out of town doing whatever they was doing back in the 90s, I was out here in Little Rock on 23rd Street repping 23$^{rd}$, banging for this 23rd Street shit in the motherfucking trenches.

--------

Fancy called me and told me that she got this old cat that she's been sexing for some time that has two rent houses around the way. She told him the business, and he said that as long as I don't fuck up his shit I can get them both today. That's right on time.

So, she gives me the address to where she's at, and I head right that way to pick her up so that we can go look at these spots. When I pull up, she's with a few niggas that I used to fuck with before I went that way. They're looking at the SS like, *who is this?* I roll the window down so they can see inside.

They're like, "Bro! I heard you was out. Why you don't come around to see your homies fam?"

I'm just looking like, *really, nigga?* I haven't seen these cats in sixteen years, ain't heard a peep from none of them, but I ain't say shit to them except, "I'll get through here later and fuck with y'all my niggas."

I look at Fancy like, *bring your ass over here.*

She jumps in the car talking 'bout, "I told them you were coming to get me, but I guess they thought a bitch was lying or some shit."

I pull off and she's looking at me all crazy and shit, so I ask what the matter is.

"Truth don't be like that. Some of them are still trustworthy."

"If you say so, but frankly I don't trust shit or nobody until I get a reason to."

The first house is on 15th and Bishop, right around the corner from Cin Park. It's a two bedroom, one-and-a-half-bath brick house with a wheelchair ramp in the front. What I like the most about the house is that it has a nice back yard that will acommodate both of my cars, and unless you come through the alley, you'll never know they're back there. The rent is five hundred a month.

The old cat just looks at me and said, "Whatever you do, don't tear my shit up! Whatever needs to be done, I don't mind coming out to take care of it."

I tell him thanks, and that I do not need to see the other location. Fancy told me all about the house, so I'd like to rent them both. We shake hands and he tells me that no deposit is required, but that I must pay both first month's rent up front and we're good. The other rental is four-seventy. I peel off a grand and hand it to Mr. Jones and the deal is done.

I'm riding away with two sets of keys and plans to get my old hood back jumping with this good gas. Baptist College right down the street.

# (Truth) Business and Pleasure

Later that day, Maria calls again, and it's a surprise 'cause I have been meaning to try and find her. The number that she called my phone from is no longer in service. I knew that all I had to do was go to the house on Lucy drive and I would be able to find her, so I wasn't too worried.

"What's up, Truth?"

"Nothing much Maria, how are you?"

"I'm fine. Are you busy right now, 'cause if not, I can have my cousin drop me off with you for a while?  I want to kick it with you today!"

I tell her that I'm not busy, and I'm not doing anything special. I told her that I had just got a new spot today and was getting ready to go do some groundwork.

I asked her, "Do you like basketball, 'cause I'm going to a college game a little bit later."

"Yeah, I like sports, but am I going to be safe with you Tyreque?"

"Yes baby, you're safe with me!"

"Ok, text me an address and I'll be right there".

I shoot her the address to the new spot on Bishop. I was just around the block fucking off when she called, so I start to walk back around there to wait for her.

As soon as I sat down on the porch an LRPD car rolls by, looking all hard at me and shit, and I'm looking back like, *boo bitch!* Then this big ass black GMC pulls up and I see Maria getting out of the passenger side with her fine ass looking all good and shit. I know that business and pleasure don't mix, but dude, this is a real live J-LO in the flesh, and the dog in me has to have a taste.

I walk out to the truck and introduce myself to the driver. "Hi. My name is Tyreque. Nice to meet you".

She takes my hand and says, "I'm Rachel. And it's finally nice to meet you too. I have heard so much about you that I feel like I know you already. However, please take care of my lil cousin."

I reassure her that Maria is in good hands, and that's a promise. I tell Rachel I hope that everything she heard about me was good.

"Good enough," she says. "That's the only reason we are where we are at this point, plus Ricky and Lou really like you."

With that I step down and close the door as she pulls off. I turn to Maria and she's standing there smiling like, *yeah, I've been talking 'bout you, so what?*

I ask her what she told Rachel about me.

"Oh, nothing really. That you are good looking and that you are always nice to me, even sweet sometimes, and that there's something about you that I just can't put my finger on. Oh, and I told her that I think I like you!"

"You think?"

"Yeah, I think".

She changes the subject.

"Have you put things inside here yet?"

"Nope. I was going to do it tomorrow."

"Good, 'cause I like decorating. Just leave that up to me, and it ain't even gone cost you that much. You got to save money to have money!"

"Right! That's how I feel exactly."

I tell her to come on, and we jump into the SS. I ask if she's hungry or if there's anything I can get her. She says that she's cool, and just happy to be out and about! Then she looks at me and asks what time is the game? I tell her in an hour or so.

We're on MLK drive headed towards the freeway. I think I want to get a suite at the Courtyard for the night. As we are pulling in at the hotel, she tells me she wants something to drink, so I ask her if she knows where the closest liquor store is. She says she does, so I peel off a fifty spot and hand it to her. I tell her that by the time she gets back, I will be ready.

"Are you staying here?" She asks.

"Yes, I am!"

"Ok, I'll call you when I'm pulling back up."

I run into the lobby and go straight to the front desk. I ask if I can get a suite for two nights.

"Yes sir! Will that be cash or credit?"

"Credit."

"Yes sir, that's going to be a seventy-five-dollar deposit, which will need to be paid in cash. I will charge your card the $170.98 for the room, and you will get the deposit back when you check out. Thank you and have a pleasant stay."

My room number is 314, and it's nice as hell. I go straight for the bed and pull the covers back on one side so it looks like only one person has been sleeping here. I go into the bathroom and unwrap the soap and drop it into the tub. I get a face towel and wet it, turn the TV on to ESPN, and I turn the sound all the way down. I turn on the radio to Power 92.3 Jams, also low. I then walk back down to the lobby and walk outside and fire up a Newport Short.

Maria pulls back in and sees me standing there. She pulls over by me and we switch spots in the car.

"How many hoes you done had up here with you?" She inquires.

"I don't get down like that, baby. I've been solo."

She looks me over and asks if we have time to go in for a few minutes.

"If you want to, yes!"

"Well, I do!"

So, I park. After finding a spot, we get out and walk into the lobby. The clerk behind the desk says, "Good evening."

I hit him right back with, "Same to you sir."

As Maria and I are waiting for the elevator, she's holding on to me, and it dawns on me that this is our first real physical contact with each other. But being as though we are both grownups, it's no secret as to what's about to go down, and I'm ready, but at the same time I'm smooth when I move. She has got to make the first move.

The elevator car finally arrives and in we go. I punch 3 and we head up. When the doors slide open, my room is right there in front of us. Key card in hand, we walk in.

Maria says, "I've got to use the restroom. I hope you've got clean towels."

I have her drink in my hand and I head over to the icebox. I had put two glasses into the freezer so that they could chill. I then pop the top on her drink, which is not a bad choice at all, Remy Martin VSOP, in the smokey green bottle!

I take the glasses out of the freezer, add three cubes of ice to each, and pour two half fingers of VSOP. When the bathroom door opens, Maria is standing there naked as the day she came into this world, and as beautiful as ever, might I add. Not a mark on her body and not an once of fat anywhere to be seen. I walk over to her and hand her the glass.

"Damn Maria! You are beautiful as hell!"

We knock back both glasses at once and head straight for the bed, tossing the rest of the sheets back. I jump out of my clothes and slide in beside her.

First a kiss, then I'm rubbing her body rough but slowly. I reach down and slide a finger into her wet, bald pussy and play with her clit. I slowly, gently nibble on her nipples, right side, left side.

Then she takes a deep breath and says, "Put it in Papi, I want to feel you inside me. Please put it in."

That Papi shit got me. I slide inside her, and it's tight and wet and it don't take me long to find the right depth and stroke. Now we're sounding like a Spanish porno movie. All I understand is, "Oh, fuck me Papi. Fuck me Papi. Oh, this dick is so good."

One minute she's speaking English and the next it's Spanish. We come at the same time. I get up and head for the shower.

She comes in and says, "That was good baby! I hope you got more for the night."

I just smile and walk into the hot spray from the shower head.

A minute later she's getting in the shower with me. We take turns washing one another's backs, and as I get done washing hers, she turns around and reaches for my dick, which instantly gets as hard as it can right there in her hands.

She soaps up a towel and runs it up and down my shaft, over and under my balls and around the head and tip, then she looks at me and says, "Ok. It's clean now."

Then she turns the water off and drops to one knee right there in front of me. She takes my whole dick inside her mouth. Man, just seeing that beautiful head between my legs going off like this is almost enough to make me blow the back of her head off. But I close my eyes and toss my head back. She must have known that she was the shit 'cause she went for broke, licking and sucking my balls, then one at a time licking and sucking the tip of the head, then deep throating me all over again.

She looks up and says, "Fuck my face Papi. Fuck my face!"

So, I start pulling in and out of her mouth slowly at first and before you know it I'm fucking her face and she is still sucking and licking and making sounds. As I feel myself about to lose control, I try to pull out but she grabs me around my waist on both sides and takes full control.

And as I start to come, she swallows it all and then sucks me dry. Right then and there, I knew that I was going to be late for the game, if I get there at all. We get out of the shower and, even though she just gave me some great head, my dick is still as hard as Japanese mathematics.

We head straight for the bed, where I take total control. Enough of the smooth nigga shit. It's time to straight up fuck. I bend her over right there in front of the bed and position her with her right leg on the bed. She's standing on her left leg, bent all the way over the bed, so I got a straight shot of nothing but pussy.

As I slide inside her she moans and says, "Fuck me Papi," and I ride her like she was a horse at the Oaklawn. As I slam in and out of her pussy, I'm smacking her ass and pulling her hair, and she's loving every minute of it.

Mid-stroke, I stop and tell her to flip over. Now I have her in the bed with both of her legs pent up looking like she's upside down, and I'm jumping in and out of her pussy. Once again, she's saying all kinds of shit in English and Spanish both mixed, and after about twenty-five minutes of this, we came at the same time again.

We take another shower and get dressed and head down to the parking deck to get into the SS and hit the slab back to MLK and Arkansas Baptist College for the game.

When we get there, we have missed the first quarter and Baptist is up by 11 points.

--------

Even though I love basketball, I'm not here for the game. I just want to spread the word that whoever wants that pressure, they can come right up to the house on 15th and Bishop and get whatever they want! 'The house with the ramp outside is what I tell all of the girls, and I let Maria say something to the guys.

So, I know that there will be a gang of dudes showing up at my door. Maybe I'll just get some girls and let them take this spot with the gas, and I'll just go to the other one, with whatever a motherfucker wants. I'm a go-getter for it so I can get it!

Maria and I hang around for an hour or so into the 4th quarter, but I'm ready to bust a move. Shit. I don't' know about her but my dick is ready to dance again. I'm like Mike Tyson in the second round. I be jabbing.

As we are walking to the car, I run into my homeboy Roddy, who works at the school.

"Damn, Cuzzo what's up?"

"Not shit Crip, how you doing?"

"I'm good just getting off. Shit. Wish I had your hands."

Shit. If he did have my hands, he'd be trying to give them hoes back. He takes a quick look at Maria and says, "Shit I don't think so."

She surprises both of us when she says, "I'm a tiger. You wouldn't know what to do with me if you had me, and even if you did your hands would be the last thing that you would want to be using."

She turns to me and says, "Baby, give me the keys. Baby, I'm waiting on you!"

I hand her the keys and she kisses me and then walks off slanging ass this way and that way.

Me and Roddy just laugh and he says, "Cuzz, you a motherfucker, you gone keep something right on your side at all times."

I tell him that she and I are just friends.

He says, "Yeah, anyway I need a half pound, and bro need a whole one."

I ask him is he sure? He assures that he is, and we agree to meet at the shop in about forty-five minutes. Once I make it to the car, I tell Maria that I have some business to take care of and ask her what she'd like to do. She says that if it's cool, she'd like to go with me. I tell her that's fine, and with that being said, we hop on the freeway headed towards Maumelle and my storage unit, so that I can grab the rest of the work that I have there.

As we are riding, she reaches into her purse and comes out with a blunt and asks can she blaze up. I tell her to go head.

Now, I'm still on federal papers, so I have not done any drugs, but at the same time my P.O. ain't really been fucking with me about no U.A. test lately. But I'm still not gone smoke. She can smoke all that she wants to. I ain't doing no tripping.

That shit be smelling so good, a nigga be about to relapse big time though. When I got locked up in the '90s, niggas was smoking Indo or Pine or some shit like that. But now these niggas be having shit with all kinds of different names and shit.

One day a lil nigga pulled up on the side of me talking 'bout, "Say, OG. I got some of that Black Superman, fifteen a G."

I just laughed to myself and said, "No, I'm cool," and pull off.

Maria looks at me and asks, "Do you smoke, Papi?"

I tell her yeah, but I also tell her about my little situation. Now she asks what did I do to go to prison so young? So, I give her a brief rundown of my story. She surprises me again and changes the subject.

"So how many girls have you been with since you've been home?"

I smile and say "I don't know. Maybe forty or fifty."

The look on her face was priceless, and I'm laughing so hard I almost flip our asses over.

She's hitting me, saying that I play too much and that I need to tell the truth. I tell her, no more like four girls in six months, and I add that pussy is not at the top of my food chain at the moment. I'm trying to stack this paper and build an empire!

--------

We pull up to the gate and I punch in my seven-digit code and the gate slides open. I pull around to my unit and use my key to gain access. I unlock the old school car and grab the book bag with the work in it out of the back seat, and lock everything back up. I head back to the neighborhood to bust the play.

Before going to the shop to meet up with my homies, I stop at the spot and go inside to put the rest of the work into the front room closet, minus the pound and a half that they want. The rest should be ok till morning. Then I think better of it, and tell myself to leave it for now, and come back and get it before I go to the hotel.

Cuzz and them are about six blocks away from the spot, but the hood be so hot, I ain't taking no chances riding with unneeded shit! It would be just my motherfucking luck to get stopped on the next block.

I pull into the parking lot right in front of the shop and I leave the car running. No one is inside but Black and Roddy, plus its 9:30. The lot is dark, so I got the weed under my arm like it ain't shit. Cuzzo unlocks the door and I walk in and hand Roddy the half and Black the whole. They bring out the brains, math is done, and cash is dropped on me! We shake hands and that's a wrap.

I get back into the car and ask Maria what she wants to do.

"It's your call Daddy. I'm cool just hanging with you."

"Is that right?"

"Yeah, that's right."

"Ok, so got a question for you."

"Go ahead and ask."

"Who are you to Ricky?"

"I'm his cousin. His mother and my mother are sisters, and Lou is their brother. Anything else?"

"Yeah. How old are you?"

"I'm 27 years old, no kids and I majored in Business Management. I have never had sex outside my race until today."

"Hold up! I didn't ask all that girl. Damn."

She laughs and says, "Well I was just getting it all out the way! Now can we please go back to the hotel and get drunk and fuck?"

I just look at her and smile, "Yea, I think we can do that."

When we pull back up into the underground parking deck, Maria says, "Listen Truth, I know that you have a girl and all that, but I like you and as long as you respect me and treat me nice we are good. I don't have a boyfriend and I don't do more than one sex partner at a time. I'm a big girl, I have my own money and I will not be a problem. I don't care what you do, but you will respect me!"

All I could say was say, "Ok," and "I like you too."

Damn it! She made me forget to stop by the spot and grab my shit. I want to go back for it, but I guess it'll be ok till morning.

We get out of the car and head into the lobby, and as we are waiting for the elevator, she's standing in front of me with her ass pressed up against my dick, which is hard as hell. I'm squeezing her ass and rubbing her tits through her shirt.

Yeah, I'm about to give her ass the business. She fucking the right nigga.

The car finally comes and we walk in. She punches the number 3 and as the door closes, we start kissing and feeling all over each other. The door opens and two girls get in as we are coming out. Right before the door slides closed, one of them winks at me or at her, I don't know for sure, but it pisses Maria off.

She says, "Boy, I tell you. Bitches ain't shit. She did that shit looking me straight in the face like I'm going to ask her if she wants to join us or something!"

By the time she's done talking, I have located the key card and we walk into the room and close the door. I open it back up and put the do not disturb sign on the door.

She turns off the TV and turns up the radio. Power 92.3 Jams is doing its thing. We are both naked and I'm making drinks. It seems like we have been doing this forever.

I hand her the glass and she takes a sip. I walk out onto the balcony to fire up a Newport. She comes out and fires up the rest of her blunt. Neither of us are saying much. We don't have to. What's understood doesn't have to be explained.

After I smoke my square, I walk over to her and take the doobey out of her hand and take a light pull. I hand it back, drain my glass, and head back inside for a refill.

As I'm refilling my glass she says, "Papi, I can't wait any longer. Come here."

I walk over to the bed and sit down. She gets on top of me and pushes me back, then she slides me inside her and starts to ride me. Slowly at first, but before you know it, she's riding me like a champ, biting her lip, and speaking in Spanish.

I roll over and get on top of her and I'm going deeper and deeper inside her. She feels so good. Her pussy is wet, and she's locking her muscles. I tell her to turn around and I enter her from the back and her fat ass is so pretty. I'm slapping her ass cheeks, left cheek, right cheek. Then I slowly take the tip of a finger and play around her asshole. Her pussy grips me like a hand.

I'm still stroking when I hear her say, "Put it in my ass Papi, but go slow."

As I push into her ass, I know that she has never done this before because it's so tight. I lose all control and cum right in her ass.

By the time I pull all the way out, I'm on E, and I feel the hit I took off her blunt, plus the Remy Martin VSOP has made its mark. I'm feeling good as hell!

I get up and walk into the bathroom to get a towel. I soap it up to wash my dick off, rinse, and re-soap it. I come back into the room to clean her. But to my surprise, she is sound asleep right there where I left her! I clean her as best I can and get into bed next to her and I fall asleep myself.

When I wake the next morning it's like 9:45 and Maria is laying next to me just looking at me.

"Hey."

"Hey yourself, Mr. Truth! When was the last time a girl told you that you was a bad motherfucker in the bed?"

I just smiled and told her, "Never. This is a first."

## Disclaimers

Ok, so let me give my disclaimers here:

First, I feel the least qualified to talk about love. I have a heart as big as Texas, but when it comes to feelings and stuff, I am ill prepared. I don't like them. I know how to push them to the side. I'd rather we sit down and rationalize things than to hack out feelings. Eew. Who does that?!?

Second, I'm going to attempt to go where no man has gone (okay, maybe one or two) but basically cracking open my feelings is a difficult task for me. Remember the day in the restaurant with my business partner Misha? I'd been working with her for about three years at that time, and that was the first time she'd ever seen an emotional response out of me (she still teases me till this day).

You get the point. I'm almost robotic. In a way I can literally hear the worst news of my life or the best news of my life and show little to no emotion.

I'm giving this disclaimer because I need for you, the reader, to understand that love, feelings and emotions are difficult for me, so you may need to use your imagination some in this chapter. I apologize ahead of time.

Carrying on...

# (Trinity) A Teenage Love Affair

I think this guy snuck me something. I mean, it had to be something. A drug in my drink, a voodoo curse (did this boy bury some draws in my backyard?). Something happened, because I know I didn't just fall in love. That was a no-no for me.

Sometimes I can't even say the word. I just call it the "L" word. All I know is I was young, beautiful, intelligent, smart, accomplished, a leader at my school, among my peers, and my ass fell in love and fell hard.

It's crazy, and I'm sure that most people who fall in love don't go looking for it, and for those who do I'm sure there is some diagnosis for that disorder.

Who would want to be in love? The heart racing, sweaty palms, the butterflies in your stomach, the feelings of insecurity. Why would anyone want that?

And on top of that, you know *love don't love nobody* - which just means love won't even love you back. It's heartless. But in spite of that knowledge and the vigilance with which I protected myself from becoming Love's latest victim, I became that very damn chick.

*Pause*

Can't you feel the warm and fuzzes in my tone? I warned you I wasn't qualified to write about love.

*Play*

So yeah, I became that girl, all in love with a guy, and a bad boy at that. How clichéd.

I almost wish that the story played out like most teenage loves do in this scenario. You know, where the boy breaks your heart and you learn the valuable lesson about bad boys and so on and so on.

Or the one where the bad boy ends up dying or something tragic like that happens (of course I'm glad this scenario didn't play out).

Or the parents oppose the affair and separate the couple by moving the girl away to live with family elsewhere.

Well, none of those things happened, and although, as in every great love story there is tragedy, this love story was and still continues to be different.

--------

This guy loved me back, totally and completely. There was no trap door or pitfall waiting for me on the other side. Just unconditional love.

In my entire 35 years of life, I cannot think of one person who has never gotten angry with me. It's strange because trust me, I can piss off the most tempered person. My daddy, who was my biggest fan, and who was the calmest person I had ever known, would get upset with me from time to time. Even he ran a close second to this young man. The sweetest, most gentle person I have ever known.

I don't remember him ever even raising his voice at me. Not once. Now this is the point where you start to think, *okay, you just found a sweet guy?*

Umm, no ma'am and no sir. On the contrary, remember I stated that he was a Crip, and not just a Crip, but an OG or leader. An original member of his set.

Those things may not mean much to you, depending on how or where you were raised, but in my hood, you have to be 'bout it for real to have that status. No game playing. A 'willing to put in work' type of person. He met the qualifications.

So no, this wasn't some softy I found out along with the Cabbage Patch Kids. He was and still is the Truth. So, let's just call him Truth.

He was extremely loyal and kind of overprotective of me but was never overbearing or controlling. I was free to be me, do me, move the way I wanted to. I didn't have to pretend with him, play hard, play soft - none of that. I could just be me.

There were some perks to being with him, I can't lie. I enjoyed the fact that people knew him, feared him, and in turn didn't mess with me. Like I said, I lived, went to school and played in a majority Bloods community and the violence was increasing in our city. No one messed with me, threatened me, or tried to intimidate me. No one.

Now, some of that was due to me being a cool female who had a lot of friends and associates. Part of it was that I kept my nose clean, wasn't messy, and didn't create a lot of drama.

But now that I'm older, I certainly give God all the praise, because He watched over and protected me. A lot of my friends didn't make it out of the '90s, and I did. But you get the idea. I was free to love and be loved, despite the violence in my community and that Truth was involved in.

Although I don't remember many details, I do remember times that we were together. It was peace in the midst of chaos. But it wasn't long before things started to catch up with him. He had stopped going to school by the ninth grade and was in and out of the county jail. He had been shot at and had been shot. His life was growing increasingly dangerous, and I found myself not feeling as free.

Although we were both fourteen, we couldn't enjoy life in that way. We were trapped in his neighborhood if we wanted to be together. Whereas we used to go to the movies and other places, the city became more and more dangerous for him. I began to drift away from him, and I believe he knew that I would.

I was becoming increasingly defiant with my parents, often sneaking out the house or skipping school to be with him. I hated getting in trouble, but I loved him and cared for him. I never knew when it would be my last time seeing him.

My parents liked Truth as a person, as he was respectful towards me and them, but they knew about his gang life and were naturally afraid for their daughter. With the tension at home, I struggled to keep up my activities and grades at school. Add to that the fact that I was losing a gang of my friends to violence. It was becoming overwhelming.

I remember one time Truth couldn't understand why I was upset about my friend getting killed, because he was a Blood. That was the only disagreement I ever remember us having.

From his point of view, he was losing his friends daily too, and was also a target. I knew that we weren't going to last because I couldn't handle it and I couldn't ask him to choose.

See, that's another thing about the way we loved each other. We were always considering each other's welfare, before consideration of ourselves.

Most girls in that situation would have made him choose the gang or them. But for me, I could not put him through that. I knew that all of his family, his friends and his protection were in his gang. I knew that I could not be for him what they could.

Just as he allowed me to be free, never dictating or smothering, I was the same with him. I just loved him for who he was. I didn't care what he was or what he did. It was an unconditional type of love.

Had that day in May not happened, the love we had would have bridged that gap for us, where no one would have had to choose.

But that's not how it happened.

--------

There was a girl in my neighborhood whom I had pretty much known my entire childhood. From first grade, we were joined at the hip. She was my best friend. Around seventh grade or so she began to get into a lot of trouble at school, and by ninth grade, she was also a member of the Crips. She and I had always remained in contact, but we grew apart in Junior High, mainly because I was more wrapped up in school and social life than she was.

We reconnected when she began dating a Crip, probably about halfway into my relationship with Truth. I don't know if it was jealousy or what, but she started to hang out with Truth and his friends more. Now in 'girlfriend 101,' you know that's a no-no. I had never even met her boyfriend, but if I had I wouldn't have been kicking it with him in her absence.

138

I would get off my school bus and they would all be at her house. Now I'm not the type of chick to compete for a guy's attention. I can easily walk away, even if it hurts. My older cousin calls it 'the gift of goodbye.'

So, for me, both of them chose their gang over me, which was cool, because in my mind, if I have to be the only one who chooses me, I will. Things became rocky between Truth and me, made worse by my growing disdain for having to have a relationship restricted to certain neighborhoods. When I begin to feel hurt, lonely, and upset, I withdraw.

For Halloween one year, I dressed as Where's Waldo, because I literally *fall back,* and you have to catch me in the wind.

As an adult I've learned that absence makes other people uncomfortable, but I can switch the game up completely. I don't know how I do it, but I can turn it off just like that. Turning it back on once it's off is a lot more difficult for me. I often feel sorry for people who get on that other side of me because it is almost always game over.

I admit I was jealous of the time he spent with her. Seeing them together was hurtful. I never saw them alone together, but it was just the fact that they were together so often. So, I withdrew. I stopped calling, stopped speaking, stopped looking in their direction when I got off the bus. In my mind

I had closed the door and put a ribbon on Truth and her. Fuck em', or so I thought.

One day I was getting off my bus and ignored them as usual. I had walked down to a friend's house but was still in plain sight. Now here goes my elephant memory. I remember it vividly.

There were a couple of guys from the neighborhood there, flirting and playing around. In my mind I know he's watching me, and I'm going to show him. I was a little more flirtatious and playful with one guy who was nobody to me. He probably didn't even have my phone number. Just a neighborhood guy. But I put on a full show. I wanted to make Truth jealous because even though my mind can trick me and others into believing I'm done - I've moved on - deuces, my heart was really hurt.

I was hurt that he was spending so much time with her and his friends. I was hurt that we were drifting apart. It hurt to think that no matter how much I loved him, I couldn't compete with his gang, his family. I was just hurt period. I couldn't admit that then but twenty years later, I know what it was.

How can you love someone and be loved by someone so perfectly, and your lives just don't fit together? And the sickening thing about our love is that were so considerate of the other that we would rather suppress our wants and desires out of respect for those of the other.

So, as I'm performing down the street, Truth, the girl, and a couple of more guys migrate to the corner, either to watch what I'm doing or to let me see what they are doing. We are about a block apart. One of the guys I was flirting with put a red cap on my head and turned it to the left, which, during that time, was a sign of disrespect to Crips. In my state of rebellion towards Truth, I didn't take it off. I figured he didn't care, so I didn't care. My hurt feelings had gotten the best of me.

The girl who I had known since kindergarten walked down and pulled a gun on me for having the hat on.

# (Trinity) Rebound

When one door closes, another one opens. That's just the way things happen in life. Life never gives you a moment to pause, to reflect, or heal. It just keeps on going.

See, part of the problem with me being so practical is that I can never just take in the good and the bad. There always has to be a reason. An explanation. Some practicality to why things happen the way that they do.

Some of my friends often say, "Well maybe it just is, Trin." Meaning maybe there's no reasoning behind things. It just is what it is. I try to subscribe to that channel at times, but I can't help who I am. It helps me to make sense of my life.

So, that door closed back in May 1993, and within weeks, another one opened.

He was tall, dark and handsome, athletic, personable and popular. He had a slew of girls that liked him. One of my friends had even shown a picture of him to me just days before I bumped into him. She was interested.

He seemed decent enough but wasn't my type. I didn't like the 'pretty boy' type; the Polo, Girbaud, Jordan wearing type of guys. They were too high maintenance. If you were that concerned about your own maintenance, how could you be concerned about me?

I just never went for that type. I liked a more rugged and down to earth guy. So, how I ended up with him I'll never know.

He had all of the qualities any teenage girl would want. He was quite a catch, and an obvious upgrade from my past relationship.

We could go out together without any worries of rival gangs. He was active in school and sports, so we ran in some of the same circles. I don't know what made me say yes to even giving it a shot with him. I guess it was feeling like it was time for something completely different. And this guy fit the bill.

It was Memorial Day, 1993, when I was visiting my aunt's house. I was a serious daddy's girl, so I was always riding shotgun with him. So, there I was in the country hanging outside with my cousins.

Yeah, I know. Crazy!

That's where I saw him. He was there with his grandmother and a couple of his younger cousins. When I saw him, I immediately placed him as the guy from the picture my friend showed me a few days before. His cousin and my cousins went to school together and were friends.

They stopped to greet each other, and I noticed him checking me out.

*pops collar*

After we all parted ways, my cousins proceeded to share their desire to hook us up. One of them was dating his cousin (who wasn't there at the time) and thought it would be cute for us to date relatives.

Later that evening, back at my house, my cousin called his cousin and somehow, he and I ended up on the phone together. The conversation was cool, so we exchanged numbers, and the rest, my friends, is history.

A wrap.

Game over.

From that moment forward, I have known no existence that he was not a part of.

# (Trinity) From Rebound to Wedding Gown

When most girls think about their wedding day, they think about flowers and dresses and bridesmaids and, oh yeah, the groom. But for me I never imagined that I'd ever get married, I just simply didn't think I was the marrying type. And not because I'm a hoe and enjoy multiple partners and could never settle for just one penis.

No, it's quite the opposite. I prefer smashing one dude for the foreseeable future because it takes too much energy during sex to be giving it out and receiving it all over the place.

I always felt that I was too selfish to get married. I like having my own shit.

But low and behold, at the tender age of nineteen, there I was with a two-year-old in tow saying, "I do," to my baby daddy/man of my dreams.

It was an eventful courtship to say the least. From that May Memorial Day in '93 to June 5, 1998, the day we were married, so much happened in so little time, including the birth of our daughter, the abortion of another child, the death of my grandmother (who was my best friend) and the death of my mother (who was my rock). As a matter of fact, my mother passed only two short months prior to our nuptials.

For all intents in purposes, our marriage was kind of shotgun in nature, and instead of the angry father, I had the proverbial shotgun locked and loaded. For whatever reason - reasons that I'm sure could successfully be explored in counseling - I was in a mad dash to the alter.

When I look back on the sense of urgency I had to marry this 21 year-old man, it's almost sickening. I've never considered myself 'that chick.' You know, the one who meets a guy on Tuesday and by week's end has the entire wedding planned out, and all of their children's names picked out in chronological order. Yeah, that chick. Yeah, um - that's never been me.

But for some reason, I was eager to marry Tony after my mom passed. I was feeling nature's call for all things 'cohabitation' several months before that. I guess since I was already a 'baby momma.' I had no long-term desire for this role. I just wanted to get married.

Sometimes it's like there are these two different, polar opposite values that are at odds within me.

Case in point: I value independence and freedom, but I don't like casual relationships with undetermined boundaries. But wouldn't that type of relationship scream independence?

When I set my mind to do something, I typically get it, and as it happened, we got married just three months after my mother passed away.

My parents weren't huge fans of Tony or our relationship. My mother felt like Tony was too controlling and possessive of me, but being young and thinking that I knew everything, I didn't heed any of her motherly intuition. I knew that Tony could be a little smothering, and during our five-year courtship we had several fights because of that. But in my juvenile mind, I really believed that having someone like him was good for me.

I felt like I needed someone to help settle me, because I would do just about anything if I felt the need to, if I was in the moment. I liked the idea that I had to answer to someone or hear somebody's mouth if I got too out of line or got into too much trouble.

I did have parents, and it's not like they just let me run wild. It's just that my mother was never really able to handle me. I was a challenge for her because we were so different in our nature. She was always the straight and narrow type of person, and I preferred the curves and edges of life. I don't know why, but despite all of her efforts to discipline me, nothing really worked.

My daddy, on the other hand, never really disciplined me. I was his baby and that's how he treated me. He would get angry with me, but it was very rare that he would even raise his voice to me, let alone a hand. So, I was spoiled, and had a lot more autonomy at a young age than what I probably should have.

My older brother, Elijah, had the same autonomy, but he has never been the risk taker child like I was. Elijah was the good child and I was the hell raiser in our home. As adults, Elijah has often told me that he felt like the ugly duckling growing up, and I was the beautiful swan, because I was more outgoing and popular.

I made good grades all throughout school, until I kind of lost interest. I had all advanced classes from the fourth grade until high school, and I was always involved in activities, cheerleading, student council, homecoming, everything. In school I was a natural leader, which was mostly a good thing, but at times I led my classmates astray, like the time I tried to burn down the school in sixth grade. But that's another story.

At one point in the sixth grade, I had so much chaos and confusion going at school that not one single girl in my class was my friend. I had nothing but guy friends, because I had pissed all of the girls off. I'd like to think I was fine tuning my leadership skills back then, and I learned quickly that I had a gift, and it was completely up to me to use that gift for good or evil.

During my years in junior high, I began to develop my skills and to be more purposeful, but by the time I made it to high school I had but almost completely given up on myself (I'll get into that later). I'm just illustrating how I was raised to paint with my own brush and how sometimes that worked for good and other times not so much.

When I met Tony, the expectations he had for me and his attention to what I was doing or not doing was kind of sexy to me. I felt like he was claiming what was his and it turned me on.

As married adults, one of my friends described my and Tony's relationship as the two Fs - fighting and fucking. Because that's all we'd done - fight and making babies - for the entirety of my twenties. Honestly, that assessment could pretty much be applied to the first ten years of our entire relationship, from dating to being a young married couple.

All of that passion and aggression turned me on. The thought that he was so messed up about me, where I'm going, and what I'm doing and who I'm doing it with, drove me crazy. My rebellious nature wouldn't let me just give in to his demanding ways, and I would fight him tooth and nail, both with my willpower and with my fists.

I remember one time I went off on Tony, and my mother came home to find Tony had blood running down his face from where I had scratched him. I remember that as one of the only times that she really felt bad for him.

I used to just think like, *damn I'm crazy.*

But as I got older, I understood that his attempts to control me and that my attempts to stand my ground were cycles of abuse.

--------

Growing up and dating, I've never been faithful in the sense that other people have. I'd have to say that the closest I've ever been to faithfulness in a relationship was with Truth.

I guess I should define what faithful means to me, since I've already explained to you that I often don't adhere to traditional rules and have never really colored inside the lines.

For me faithfulness in a romantic relationship is when I'm only sleeping with one person (which is 90% of the time with me), and I'm not entertaining or actively interviewing my mate's potential replacement (um… yeah, so like 15% of the time maybe).

I'm from the school of thought where every car always needs to have a spare. You know, just a little something something just in case your main car gets to acting up.

That was me the majority of my dating life, and again, I never thought that I'd get married. I had a number of guys with whom I kept company. Guys love sexy, beautiful, confident girls, so I always had my picks and chooses, and I'm not really a choosy person.

You don't have to be 6"1' with a six-figure income if we have a good vibe, and that's pretty much all I need. Do I like you? That's pretty much all I need to know to get you in the rotation.

As to getting into bed with me, now, that's something else. When it comes to sex, I am very picky. I'm what I've learned in adulthood is a 'demi-sexual.' What that means is that I have to feel an emotional connection with you to sleep with you.

And of course, I've explained that I ain't the most emotional chick walking these streets, so my body count is super low compared to many other women my age. I've only slept with approximately five guys and no girls (she don't do girls at all) my entire life. I may have gotten started early, but my mileage is low, and of those five guys, maybe only three of them were more than a few times, and only two were men who could live inside me, as they were around me that much.

Outside of that, I like to keep my pussy a well-kept secret.

So back to this concept of faithfulness.

Truth was probably the only guy who got that from me, because when we were together, I was truly happy, plus, he was crazy, so I didn't want to put anyone else in danger.

I still had guy friends, and he never tripped on me about that, ever. It was kind of like we respected each other's personal space, or maybe he just knew he had me gone over him. I don't know, but he was the only guy I dated. I didn't have any other guys in my rotation or on back order.

I didn't have a backup plan with him because I never thought that I would need one. But when it did end, I was on the prowl, and when I met Tony, I just added him to the roster. When I began dating Tony, I was already sorting through other guys and kind of putting them in pecking order, based on who had the most money or who looked the best.

Whereas before Truth, I wasn't as concerned with those things, this time around any guy in my life had to benefit me, because love was a thing of the past. So, I put Tony at the top of my list because he looked good and could dress his ass off and he was papered up.

Hell, he put himself at the top of the list because he literally spoiled the fuck out of me. Jordan's, Tommy Hilfiger, Girbauds, jewelry, necklaces, bracelets, and at one point he had spelled out his entire name on my hand in gold rings!

*Biiiiiittttttcccccchhhhh!*

Literally, whatever I wanted I got, and I had never been a label whore before or the least bit materialistic like that, but damn, he got me hooked. He literally bought and paid for my young ass. I was his.

--------

I had loved Truth before and I was now in love again, and the biggest difference between the two loves was that now, the love I got in return for my love, I had to earn. I had to work to get him to fall in love with me, and I had to work to keep it, and when I got tired of working or couldn't work anymore, the nature of his love would change.

It's like I had to meet expectations or fill a quota, and if I didn't, Tony could quickly change from a loving benefactor to a verbally abusive tyrant.

I didn't really see it like that at the time, though. Initially, I felt like well, this is my man and he does so much for me, so if he doesn't want me to have guy friends I can understand.

Then it would be well, if he doesn't want me to go to this party or this event with my friends, I get it. Why would a man want his girl out all the time. But then it became 'why are you always with this hoe girlfriend, or why did you not call me as soon as you got home?'

For a while I thought it was cute, and I had just chalked it up to his being whipped. He claimed that I was his first, and I'm not sure how true that is, but I definitely know that I was more experienced than he. I had had almost a full year of learning how to make love to my man and learning how to please.

I loved pleasing my man, so if you were my man you got all benefits pretty much anytime you wanted them. I'm very sexual, so I'm sure I was doing some things to him that he had never had done before. My little cocky ass was like, *yeah, he's just sprung, so that's why he's acting like this.*

But as the relationship progressed, it got worse, and I rebelled, because that's what I do. I had a few on my team of reserves, but Tony took up so much of my time and space that it was hard to keep up with them, plus I wasn't giving out no pussy, so it was only conversation and flirting with the boys on the bench, at that point.

I began to feel a little stuck and caged in. If I haven't mentioned it yet, I'm a Leo. In other words, a Lion, and we don't do cages well. My claws came out, hence the blood-down-the-face episode.

Since the onset of our dating relationship, twenty-five years ago, Tony and I haven't had one solid year of faithfulness or peace.

# (Truth) Plans in Motion

I'm getting out of the bed and Maria says, "I have already called a few places that will deliver everything that you need to the house. For $2,500, the whole house will be taken care of. And I took the liberty of ordering everything in black; everything in the bedroom will be black except the curtains, and they will be in blue! Now all you got to do is give me the go ahead, or we can look at a few places, if you want to."

I tell her that I trust her and that it's cool, whatever she picked out, so we can just go to the spot and wait for the delivery truck. She gets on the phone and tells the man that it's a go. She asks me for the address to the spot on Bishop, then she turns to me and says, "Papi, will you go get that bag out the trunk for me please?"

I'm like, "Sure," but I'm thinking, *what bag in my trunk?*

I threw on my clothes to run down to the car, pop the trunk and grab the bag to bring back up to her.

She says, "Thanks boo," and starts pulling out clothes and shoes and brand-new toothbrushes and toothpaste and all kinds of shit. I mean, Shorty was ready!

I pick out a toothbrush and go into the bathroom to brush my teeth and wash my face, while she walks in and gets into the shower. I'm a hood nigga on a mission, so being in the same clothes for a while don't mean shit to me right now, but I do plan on stopping by my mom's crib to see if I got something that I can slide into over there. I ain't going home till tomorrow, 'cause I know what that's going to be like.

Maria gets out the shower, and I run from the bathroom, 'cause if I don't we'll be fucking on the bathroom floor.

I head to the car. While I'm sitting in the car waiting for her to come down, I count out $2,500 and put the other $2,900 in the console. It'll be going into the safe when I get to the house.

Maria comes down and gets in, I hand her the cash and we pull off for the hood and the spot on Bishop.

As soon as we pull up, I get out and go straight into the house to see if my shit was still there. It's right where I left it, so I close the door and go back outside to find Maria on the porch rolling up a blunt.

She looks up and says, "Truth, you a real cool laid back kind of dude. I don't believe half the shit I have heard about you! But then again there's something in your little black eyes that says you are a cold-blooded killer, and believe me, just because I'm a girl don't mean that I don't know what I'm talking about." She takes a puff of the blunt and continues. "Truth, I heard your name before we met. Your homeboy Dinky used to try to get at me, but I wouldn't fuck with him. He was always talking about you though. I saw him a few times at my uncle Lou shop. My first time seeing you was the night that he got killed. You had on all blue and you had two girls with you and some little nigga with all red on."

I sat in silence and let her continue.

"I heard the females talking about you all on your dick and shit, saying how the Crip hood was gone be popping again now 'cause you're out. That night at my house for my cousin's party, I wasn't gone say nothing but when you started coming on to me, I said, *what the fuck?* Plus I know can't too many of these tired ass Little Rock bitches hold my bra strap when it comes to dudes! And like I said before, you are the first guy that I have ever had sex with that was not Mexican."

Before I could keep the conversation going, the truck pulled up, and the movers started doing their thing. Maria was right there calling all the shots, so I just went back to the car and started thinking of my homeboy and brother Dinky.

It hurt me to my soul, 'cause even though I wasn't calling him up there to help me and Lucky, I still can't help but think that if I hadn't made that call, Cuzzo would still be here right now. I say a silent prayer, wipe a tear away from my eye and say, "I'm sorry, brother."

I was still sitting there when Maria walked up to the passenger window and said, "Ok, daddy. Come check it out and see if you like it."

Shit looked real nice. One could tell that it had a female's touch to it. I look in the bedroom and almost fall out. You can see your reflection off both walls facing the bed, as well as the ceiling!

Maria just looks at me with a wicked ass smile and says, "A bitch better be something special to put her ass down on this bed."

Then she smacks me on my ass and walks out the room saying, "Now come on and drop me off at the house so I can take care of some of my business. Plus, I got something for you! Oh, yeah. Are we on the same page as far as our little 'situationship' goes?"

I tell her of course we are and walk her out to the car.

When we get outside and start walking towards the SS, a car pulls up and I see that it's my homeboy Malcolm. He's a Blood, but he's still my nigga all the same, and I'll put a brick in the hospital with a rock for him.

Malcolm is real laid back, and I don't know anyone that can out hustle the nigga when it comes to that bae!

"I thought that was your car nigga. Where you been at?" Malcolm says. "The word is you got that thraxxx and all my lil niggas is looking for that shit."

"That's what's up bro. Tell them to come by the house with the ramp, and I got them, bro."

"Ok, my nigga. That's what's up."

--------

Maria and I are smashing down Arch Street on the way to her house, and then I'm going back to the spot to bag up some of this gas. It's time to get this spot jumping.

When I pull up, she tells me to hold up. Tells me that she needs to go get something that she has for me. She runs into the house and comes back out with a brown paper sack and in it is five pounds of cush.

"My cousin left some shit here for me to hold, just in case you called. I already told him that you came for this, but I paid for it myself and I want you to have it. I know you just got out and shit. And since I've been kicking it with you, I know that you gone make it happen. You don't owe me nothing. Just get back where you feel like you should be, Papi, 'cause I know that these niggas out here are not ready for The Truth!'"

I ask, "You sure?"

She turns and walks away saying, "I'll be by the spot later."

I head right back to the spot. I stop at Crip 6 and get three boxes of zip lock bags and a few hundred of them dime sacks, and twenty bags. Back at the house, I'm bagging up eight pounds, all zips and half zips, then the other three all the way down to three point fives.

After finishing up, I take a walk through the house, and I realize that it looks really good in here! You can't tell that it's going to be a spot. It looks lived in, and will soon smell that way, too.

While I'm inspecting the house, the doorbell rings. Looking out the peephole, I see my nigga Malcolm. I open up and tell him to come on in. He says that his relative is outside and he needs that gas.

He says, "I see you got it. What's your numbers?"

I tell him the number and put most of it up, and then I tell him to tell his boy to come in and look for himself.

He comes in and says, "Boy, I smell that shit. How much for two slabs? And if it smokes as good as it smells, I'll be back, 'cause I got a gang of niggas trying to get straight. If you give me a nice number where I can give them a little play, I can get rid of at least ten of them tonight, on Blood."

Malcolm is like, "Hold up nephew. I told you my nigga is Cripping, so hold up with that 'on  Blood' shit. It ain't called for!"

"It's cool bro." I say.

The little one says, "I didn't mean no disrespect Big Bro. That's just how I talk."

I tell him no disrespect was taken, and that he can say whatever he wants to say as long as he running through 10 a night. I drop my price for him to $150, so he getting them for $3,450.

"Bet," he says, and takes my number and the two slabs, and he and Malcolm leave. Malcolm stops and tells me that he'll be back just to chill and fuck off a little bit. I tell him that's cool, and they dip.

I go back into the bedroom and put the money into the dresser and go back up front to see where I laid my phone down. As I'm walking up the hall, it starts to ring. When I get to the display, I see that it's my baby momma.

"Hello…"

"Don't bother bringing your black ass up in here. You act like we don't live together. It's been two days since we last saw you, with your cheating ass!"

"Baby don't act like that. You know what I'm out here doing and why. All you thinking about is me being with another bitch and I'm telling you ain't no hoes on my mind. I'm trying to stack this paper up for our family! I'll be home in the morning."

"Well, me and the kids will be gone unless you bring your ass home right now."

"Baby I can't right now. Your homeboy Malcolm is on his way over here, and he bringing some young niggas that want this gas."

"Truth, I didn't want you back out there selling shit and trying to keep up with the Jones. You know all them Feds need is to hear your name in some shit, and they'll be kicking doors down all over the city trying to lock your black ass back up!"

"I know baby, and it ain't gone be much longer."

"Yeah, whatever. What's the combination to your safe?"

I smile and say wouldn't you like to know and hang up the phone laughing.

I got off the phone and I noticed that it smells like gas all over this little house, so I make a mental note to stop buy CRIP 6 and get something for the smell.

My phone rings again and its Mack.

"What up bro?"

"Not shit. At the spot. What you got going?"

"Nothing. Trying to give you them shoes back and get another pair."

I give him the address and he says, "Hey bro, yeah, I got my homeboy with me. His name is Lewis Johnson, but we call him MG. He's cool, and I will personally vouch for him."

I tell him okay, and that a friend of his is a friend of mine. So, while I'm waiting on them to get here, I pull out the last of the pounds of skates I got left, and I'm thinking that this shit is taking over. Crack what?

# (Trinity) The Truth

It had been several months since I saw Truth that day in the restaurant. It's not that I hadn't thought about him, because I had, but just as I did when we were kids, I was able to tuck those thoughts away.

Hey, my motto has always been 'I don't let grass grow under my feet, I am not a tree', so in the midst of growing a thriving therapy practice and raising the future Baracks and Michelles, I had my hands full. But something in the back of my mind knew that that day would not be the last time I heard from Truth.

I was returning from a trip out of town, a basketball tournament I'm sure, because you've got to be the all-around mom of the year, participating in every activity with your cubs.

I had made it to my office, and I had a message from an old student of mine from my earlier years working in the school district. It wasn't odd that my old students or clients would track me down to ask for referrals, or even to give me an update on their current lives. But with this particular student, it was different.

I talked with her numerous times over the years, but somehow, I knew that Truth was behind this call.

How he even knew that she and I knew each other, I'll never know. But low and behold the call was made, and he asked her to ask me if I'd be willing to talk to him.

Almost as if I had stepped out of my body and someone else took over, I gave her my office phone number to give to him. No hesitations, no further thought put into it, just sure, here's my number. Within what seemed like a few seconds, my phone was ringing.

I'm freaking out.

*Should I answer? What will I say? OMG, I'm on the third ring. I have to answer it, because if don't, I can't call him back.*

"Hello," was the only word that I got out of my mouth before he took complete control of my mind, body and spirit right there over the phone.

Now, I know I've explained to you that I am a strong woman, not to be played with, but, for whatever reason, the sound of his voice, after all these years, left me speechless.

It's a good thing that he did take over the conversation, because we would have just been enduring the silence if he hadn't. The way he took over, it seemed as if he had waited his entire life to speak these words.

I will never forget the urgency in his voice, I could only understand like, every third word, because he was talking like he had just downed ten Red Bulls and a speed ball. I was able to make out that he was sorry for how we had ended our relationship back in the day. He told me that he still loved and missed me, and that he thought about me almost every day that he was in prison. He told me that he had just been released not too long before we had seen each other in the restaurant, and that in that short time he had witnessed his best friend's murder.

I think I managed to tell him that I had forgiven him, and that I understood how things were back when we were young. I managed to spit out that I was married with three children. I know I must've said that, because he went silent for a few moments while he processed my words.

He asked me if he could see me so he could tell me the things he had wanted to tell me for all these years, and do it face to face. He didn't wait for me to respond. He told me that if I would see him, I could get his number from his cousin and let him know.

Just like Truth to bare his soul to me, leave all this shit at my feet, and then throw the ball in my court. We exchange goodbyes and hang up, and I'm frozen right there in that moment.

It's been several years since that conversation, and I'm still frozen.

It took me a few hours to get his number and work up the nerve to call. We agree to a date three days from now which means I have exactly three days to fake my own death.

I started thinking.

*Why did I not call somebody first, somebody older and wiser, maybe my brother? He would have certainly told me not to return the call.*

Well okay, I made that mistake, but I'll call him now so that he can help me figure out how to get out of this hole that I have dug for myself. He can reason with me and tell me how much I don't need to meet with him, how the past is the past, and what good could possibly come from this meeting? He could warn me that I haven't seen this man in years, that he had been in prison for most of his adult life, and just might be dangerous. He could use some scare tactic about how ex's often hunt down old girlfriends to exact revenge on them.

*Yes, that's what I'll do*, I thought. *I'll call my older, wiser brother and he will help me to get this madness out of my head.*

"Hello."

"Yes."

"Hey, can you talk?"

"Sure."

I proceed to spill my guts to him. I'm sure at this point I'm sounding just as urgent as Truth had when he first called me. After I get it all out, my brother, bless his heart, in all of his brotherly wisdom says, "Well, maybe he just needs closure. I think you should hear him out."

*What the hell! Was that his advice?*

As a parentless child, the closest thing that I have to a parent is my older brother, even though we are only separated by three years. He's always been the more sound, solid and stable of the two of us. He's the calm, level-headed one, and I'm the wild child.

It's not that he gave me his blessing because he knows me well enough to know that I'm going to do what I want to do, but it was his lack of resistance to the idea that really surprised me.

Up until these very moments, I didn't fully understand what Truth and I had in the past. I knew that I had loved him, and that he was my first love. I knew that in terms of passion and friendship and love, we were the ideal picture of teenage love.

I don't remember us ever arguing or fighting. All I really remembered is that it didn't work out between us because of his involvement with his gang, and my desire to be carefree, not burdened with the responsibility of being an OG's girlfriend. All that, plus having a friend who, for whatever reason, didn't want to see us together.

Bam. Issa break-up.

Fast forward a little. I remember that although we had broken up, he would still call me from time to time. He would write me letters when in jail and send me pictures that probably another guy had drawn, and he would call.

By this time, however, I had gotten a taste of what life was like when you could go anywhere you wanted without fear of getting shot because of who you were with. I was hurt, but I was also emancipated. For a young fly girl such as myself, the sky was the limit.

But I couldn't help feeling that I was abandoning Truth. Our relationship was different from any other that I had had before. It wasn't just that he loved me. It was that he also needed me and needed me in a way that a newborn baby needs it's mother.

I knew what made him tick, even at an early age, and I knew how to handle him and manage him.

In the streets, he was a force to be reckoned with. A beast. But to me, he was a little kitten who needed love, nurturing and affection. And at times, to be popped on his tail if he got out of hand.

I remembered those things about us, and now that I'm older, I understand things a little bit different. I forgave my fourteen-year-old self for walking away from him. In essence, I was throwing away love. I understood what I would have had to give up to keep that love, back then, and I also know now that you can never really throw true love away.

--------

Truth had re-entered my life and turned it upside down. Within three days I'd be facing my past, my Truth - head on - and I couldn't help but be a little afraid. It crossed my mind that this meeting would not even take place, and I was working myself up for nothing. You know how guys are. They say one thing and then do another.

I was sure his mouth had written a check that his ass had no intention of cashing, right? Wrong! He didn't even make it three days before he called me. I gave him an address where he could meet me.

I started to have him meet me at my office. It was a Sunday night, so no one would be there. But for some reason I felt like that might be too formal. I mean, in some ways he was kind of like my first client.

I'd often get calls from him or his friends or family when he would get angry and no one could talk him off the ledge. We always had a way with each other, where when one would talk the other would listen. We were just like that with each other. Not much had changed.

So, instead of meeting him at my office, I gave him the address of my best friend's apartment. As luck would have it, I was housesitting for her that evening. She had never met

Truth before, and up until his reappearance in my life, I'm sure I hadn't told her much of him. But as my closest friend in my adult life, she knew of the pain and mistreatment in my marriage.

She also knew that my agreeing to meet Truth was a slippery slope, but nevertheless, she was okay with me meeting him there.

--------

Some moments in time you just never forget. They linger in your mind like a weird aura hanging over you. Such a time was that Sunday night in July. I met him up the street to escort him to her apartment, and he followed me. When I had gotten out of the car and stood there waiting for him to silence the roaring engine on his old school, I felt like I was thirteen again, right there in the parking lot in my cheerleading outfit, waiting on a boyfriend who had no business even knowing how to drive, let alone having access to a vehicle.

When he got out of the car, the way he looked at me was as if Cupid himself had struck him with an arrow. He grabbed me and hugged me. I did not expect that at all.

I don't know what I expected. Maybe a firm handshake and from me, "Hi, Truth, I'm your grown up first love Trinity.".

No, no words could ever describe the feelings, looks, and hugs exchanged in that parking lot.

After we let each other go, which felt like an hour later, he asked me if I felt that electricity. Funny, but what I felt I wouldn't quite describe as electricity. Anxiety, maybe. A bit of weakness and nausea.

Either way, I was here now in the arms of a love that I once knew so well - that I never thought I'd see again - with my heart racing a thousand miles a minute.

He looked pretty much the same as I remembered him, except that he had more weight on him. He wasn't a skinny kid anymore. I'm sure he had tattoo's back then, at least a few, but now he had them pretty much covering every available space on his arms, and even a few traces of tear drops underneath his eye (we know what that typically means).

I'd remembered him to be a little taller than I, but at this moment in time my head met him at his chest. I'd noticed these few things, but honestly, he could've been missing an eyeball and two limbs and it wouldn't have changed what I felt in that moment.

We went into the apartment, and I don't really remember all that was said. But I remember being on that couch, in that apartment on that Sunday night, in emotional heaven.

I told him about the loss of my parents, and my tumultuous marriage to the man that I met just weeks after our breakup. I told him about my career as a therapist, and how I felt our relationship and seeing the things that he went through as a kid prepared me to go into my field.

I spilt all of my proverbial tea that Sunday evening. I don't know if it was nervous energy or pent-up frustrations or what, but I did an emotional dump on this man. This man that I had not laid eyes on in almost twenty years.

I cried and cried and cried.

Later he told me that he was crying also that night, but I couldn't tell you if he was or wasn't, because for once in my adult life, it was my time to talk and someone else's to listen.

I shared so much with him that night that I literally felt naked in front of this man. I imagined how Adam and Eve might have felt in the Garden of Eden prior to their transgression. I imagine that they were unaware, and perfectly comfortable with being naked before one another. That's the naked that I felt.

Opening up to Truth felt as natural as eating at my grandmother's kitchen table. It didn't surprise me until after the evening was over, and I had to splash cold water on my face to realize that this was not a dream.

We sat and talked for hours, my head on his chest, as he passed his fingers through my curly hair, the two of us lying across my girlfriend's couch, as if this was our regular Sunday night routine.

--------

I don't remember if he said goodbye first or I did. I don't remember if I walked him to his car or if we had a parting hug. All I remembered is that my life had been touched and changed that Sunday night in a way that I would never really be able to put into words or explain to another.

My heavy sobs and tears in my best friend's bathroom mirror woke her from her sleep.

"Are you okay?" She asked.

All that I could utter was an almost inaudible, "No." We talked for a little while, and because I was aware that she had work and school the next day, I thanked her for her hospitality and told her that I'd call her in the morning.

I made it to my car, eyes still puffy from crying, and I confidently found just the song I needed to hear to steer me to the house - Maze, featuring Frankie Beverly's, "I Wish You Well."

Frankie Beverly's smooth voice sang, "I wish you well girl, I hope you find your truth. I wish you well girl, I want the same things too."

I've always had an old soul, as the old folks used to say, and my musical selections confirmed that fact. No song could tell a story, explain a truth or describe a feeling as well as an old-school R&B song.

There is literally no emotional situation that has ever existed that hasn't been revealed in the lyrics of a song.

I imagined that this would be the last time I heard from Truth. He and I had gotten the much-needed closure that my brother had suggested we needed, and there was no longer any need to continue on.

He had shared with me details of his current relationship with the mother of one of his sons. His son had only been a baby when he began his fourteen-year incarceration in federal prison. Although he and they had not stayed in contact the entire time of his incarceration, they had reconnected prior to his release and were trying to be a family.

I respected that.

Up until this time, I had never consciously spent any intimate time alone with any other woman's man, husband, or boyfriend. I didn't get down like that, because I respected other people's relationships, and I had always had my own, or else perfectly fine single guys who were interested in me. I've never felt the need to compete.

So, in my mind and my heart, I said goodbye to this man on this Sunday night. I had cried all of my tears. I had said everything that I could think to say. We had an unspoken agreement that there could be nothing further between us.

I'm riding and singing and reminiscing. My phone buzzes:

Truth: I love you Trinity, I always have and I always will.
Trinity: I love you too, Truth.


As I make my way into my driveway, I pull myself together as best I can so as to not alert anyone of my emotionally exhausted state of mind. I step into my home. The house is dark, and the kids are sleeping. I step in my bedroom and cut the light on. My bedroom is empty.

It must be another late night for my husband.

# (Truth) Home is Where The Heart Is

I call my little cousin and ask her if she knew Trinity. She says yes, and that they are very close, and why am I asking? I give her a bullshit run down and ask if she can call and set up a meeting for me. She said she would give it a try and call me right back.

So, I'm sitting around waiting on either Mack, Malcolm or my little cousin to call, and I'm thinking of all the shit in the world that I could be doing.

*Why did I have to turn back to these streets and this cold ass game that don't love nobody, no matter how you add it up?*

I think about all my family members that are locked up doing life, or a stretch that they can't do; Little Mike Walker, my cousin, doing life in the ADC, my uncle, David Robinson, doing life in the federal prison system, and my brother Leeland Robinson doing fifty-five years in the federal pen 'cause of a bunch of hoe ass niggas that couldn't do they time like men.

This government is so fucked up, and it ain't just the white man. It's the black man too; killing they own and any other motherfucker that they can fuck over.

My thoughts are interrupted by the ringing of my phone. It's my little cousin calling back to tell me that Trinity said that she would love to meet with me and talk! She gave me a number and said that I should call, and we can arrange a time and a place to meet up.

Now for some reason I'm scared to call, and it's crazy, 'cause people see me as some kind of lady's man, yet here I am scared to make a call and set up a time just for conversation.

This is Trinity! Not some random chick. She is my first real love and my first everything. She left an impression on me way back then. I mean, I think I have loved this woman my whole life.

I have been so hard on other females because they couldn't compare to this woman. And it seems like every time I think of her or talk to her it makes me think about my life and the way that I'm living. There's something about this woman that makes me want to be a better me and lead a better life.

I make the call, and it seems like it took forever, but it was really only three rings. She picks up, and as soon as I hear her voice my whole train of thought just stops, 'cause I don't know what she's going to say, or how she feels about seeing me or talking to me for the first time in over fifteen years.

I later found out that she was just as scared as I was, and it was making us both crazy. The conversation lasted for about an hour, and we caught up on all kinds of things. But what was more surprising to me was the fact that sex never crossed my mind, but love was never far from it!

For some reason, I know that with this woman is where my heart belongs.

We set a day and a time to meet up. She told me that she had to hang up, but that she was looking forward to our meeting in three days. She also said it was good seeing me that time, even though both of us were scared like we had seen a ghost, and that she probably feels the same as I do. I must confess though, that when she told me that she was married and that she had three kids, it kind of hurt me a little bit or disappointed me. I really don't know.

--------

I got saved by the doorbell ringing. When I open the door, I see that it's Mack and MG, and Malcolm is sitting out in his car. Mack asks me who's out there and I tell him that that's just Malcolm, one of my true Blood homies, and I wave for Malcolm to come into the house. So, we all fall in, and Malcolm goes straight to the back of the house, while Mack, MG and I take care of business up front.

MG wants a pound and a half, and Mack wants the rest. That would usually be a cool $30,000, but Mack is my brother

178

and MG is his, so I give them a cool price at $24,000. I tell them the price and they step aside to discuss.

MG asks can he try a hit, and I say of course, 'cause I know my shit is good. He pulls out a bowl and smashes a shard into the stem and gets his roll on, and then blows out a million bucks worth of smoke and starts to count out his money. Mack does the same.

I tell them that I want my bag back as they were headed out the door. Malcolm comes into the room and says, "Boy, you eating off that shit, huh?"

I just smile and take the money to my room. I'm still thinking some of the same thoughts from earlier, and I'm like, *Truth what the fuck are you thinking about?* But at the same time, I gots to get this money.

I haven't been home in two days, and I got $21,800 that needs to be put into the safe.

Malcolm and I sat around talking shit and drinking Remy V and playing Xbox One 2k12. His freaky ass got some little chick on the phone and he looking at me like, *can I give her the address?*

I don't care and tell him that he gone have to hold down the fort, 'cause I'm going home to face the music. I know my baby momma ain't gone have shit good to say to me, and she might even put her hands on me. But hey, these are the games that a nigga like to play.

As I'm leaving, I tell Malcolm to put his car into the back yard and for him to make sure that he tells his little chick to do the same, and call me in the a.m., because it's Friday and the college gone jump for this loud pack. I give him a three and a half for his little chick, and I head on to the crib.

--------

As soon as I call my house, my baby girl answers the phone like she's my woman or something, talking about, "We ain't seen you in two days! If you ain't here by nine o'clock we putting your stuff outside."

I bust out laughing and say, "Ok, baby girl. I'm sorry," and I tell her that I'm on my way home right now and will be there in 15 minutes. I ask her to not put my stuff outside.

She says, "Well you better get here then. My momma wants to talk to you."

She passes the phone to her momma, who gets on the phone laughing and talking about, "Did she just say what I thought she said?"

I'm like, "Yeah, she told me if I don't get here my stuff is going outside. Now why is my seven-year-old saying something like that?"

"I don't know. She must've heard me talking to my friend on the phone and I was telling her that if you didn't get here, me and Sweetie was putting your shit out!"

I tell her, "Well, don't touch my shit. I'll be there in ten minutes. I'm on the bold."

She tells me I'm right on time, 'cause she cooked about thirty minutes ago; roast beef, mac n cheese, green beans and potatoes, with peach cobbler on the side.

"I'll put you a plate in the microwave."

I tell her okay and that I'll be right there.

She warns me not to think that this is over. "Truth, you ain't had your black ass home in two days!"

"Look woman! I done told you what's up." I tell her "I'm out here trying to get this paper. I don't want my kids growing up the way I did. I'm taking these chances so in the long run, we can sit back and relax!"

With that, I hang up the phone, 'cause I'm in our neighborhood.

I hit the button on the garage, double doors go up, I pull in and hit the button, doors go down, and then I get out the car.

My seven-year-old is standing there with her hands on her hips talking bout, "I almost forgot I had a daddy."

"Well, you sure do."

I pick her up and head into the house. Picking her up ain't as easy as it used to be 'cause she's growing up fast, and I see that hanging out with her mom ain't getting it. Some little nigga gone have his hands full with this one.

The food is good, and it feels good to be home, but it also feels like I'm back in jail or something. I don't know what it is. My baby momma is clean and cool, for the most part, but then again, it's hard dealing with her and her mood swings. She's yelling at the kids all the time. The kids and I be looking at her like she done lost her rabbit ass mind!

Like, why do you give your kids their own rooms and then won't allow them to close the door? Or she makes a big deal about them getting shit out of the refrigerator and this and that.

Once I'm done eating, I step back out into the garage and get the little bag out my back seat, then I close the doors and lock the car up. I head straight for the closet in my bedroom. As soon as I get the safe open, my baby momma comes in.

"Truth, you know you've been with some hoe. Why won't you just tell me who the bitch is? I will find out and when I do, I'm going to beat the bitch's ass and then I'm gone come for you!"

I'm like, "Look here, I don't have time for this shit. I have told you a thousand times I've been out there grinding."

I pull the twenty-one-something thousand out and flash her ass with them stupid knots, then I say, "Now will you leave me alone about some bitch?"

Then she switches it up and say, "Well let me see your phone."

"Hell to the nall! I don't need you all in my personal business. My phone is my business. You don't see me asking for your phone that you keep stuck up in your face all the time."

"Cause you know I don't do nothing! But keep on fucking with me Truth, and I'm gone fuck you smooth the fuck up!"

I'm like yeah, yeah and keep right on counting my chips while putting it into the safe. She leaves me alone, finally, and gets on the phone with one of her bullshit ass friends. I hear them talking about me though!

*Boy, I can't wait to get the fuck up out of here! I'm saying to myself.*

Now don't get me wrong. I love my baby momma, but too much damage is done and she don't trust me for shit. She done put the police in my life too many times. We both know that it's over. I guess we been sticking shit out cause of the kids.

With that thought, I go into my son's room and he's like, "Dad, they been mean to me. Every time you be gone they be mean to me. Eating ice cream but won't give me none, and my granny came and got Sweetie and bought her the new J's, but didn't get me nothing!"

I tell him don't trip. "We gone go hook you up tomorrow!"

He says okay, and then asks me to play Madden 13 with him. For the next hour I'm getting my ass handed to me by my son, and he's feeling himself. Then I hear my baby momma calling me to come here, so I tell my son to go on and get ready for bed. I hug him and tell him not to worry. He will have the new J's tomorrow.

"Okay, Dad, I love you, and thanks."

"I love you too, son."

As I walk into the bedroom, she's watching this bullshit ass ID Channel, and it's some crazy ass bitch on here whose done killed her husband and her three kids. She's telling the police that someone broke into the house and just started shooting her family, but she ran and hid from them. I'm thinking like, *is this crazy ass bitch thinking about doing something to me and these kids?*

"Why you always watching this bullshit? I ask her.

"I don't know, maybe I'm thinking about killing your ass."

I grab the remote and switch that shit to Sports Center. We sit there ignoring each other.

Then she says, "Truth, I love your no-good ass, but you gone make me hurt you about playing with my heart!"

We end up talking all night, and I think we came up with a understanding that we were just gone be friends and co-parents.

The next morning, I wake up and they're gone. She left a note telling me that I left the safe open, so she got out enough money to pay both of my car notes and the rent. She also said that she was gone stop by the mall and get Devon some new J's and a few other things. She also cooked breakfast and put mine into the microwave, so I eat and take a shower and get dressed.

I go to the storage and pull out my old school. The weekend is here, and I'm about to hit the town and turn up like a motherfucker!

I make a call to Trinity and ask if I can see her. She laughs and says that we've got a date set already. I tell her that I can't wait that long. She says that it's just a few more days. I tell her again that I can't wait, then she laughs, and says that she was about to call me anyway and let me know that she was going be at her homegirl's house housesitting, and that if I wanted to I could come over tonight so that we can talk. She gave me the address and I told her that I'd see her later tonight.

Then all of a sudden, I got spooked.

Why?

I don't know, but there's something about this woman that does something to me. Just the thought of her makes me feel like a little schoolboy, in love for the very first time in his life. I second-guess my lifestyle, and it just really makes me want to do better! It's like I know that I should be doing something more with myself.

We will talk tonight and see how we feel after all this time.

--------

I called Trinity and ask her which way I turn once I enter the complex. She tells me right, then left, and I should see her standing by the big green dumpster.

When I see her, it's like everything else around me just stops. I love this woman, and I have loved her all of my life.

When I was in prison, I had the time to think about my life and how I wished it would have turned out, and I always found myself thinking about Trinity.

I'd be saying to myself, *I wonder where she is and what she's doing.*

I could not explain this feeling that I had back then, and that I'm feeling again.

At the very moment I'm walking towards her, I realized that the feeling was love. That's all it ever was, and all it ever will be!

She's standing there before me looking and smelling good, and when we hugged, I almost passed out right there in her arms!

Then she says, "Hi Tyreque. Or should I call you Truth?"

"You can call me whatever you want to call me as long as you call me tomorrow and then the next day and the day after that!"

She laughs and says, "I see you are still a charmer."

All I could do was look at her and smile. She led me into her homegirl's apartment. I'm checking her out. I can't believe that, after almost sixteen years, I'm holding the hand of the woman of my dreams.

As we enter the apartment, she asked if I wanted something to drink. I declined, and we sat down and started to talk. She gave me a run-down of her life since we were last together.

She told me things that she would dare not mention to other people. She told me that it felt good to have someone that she could trust and let it all out to, and of course I'm a good listener!

Then it was my turn to do the talking. At some point she began to cry, and it didn't take me long to cry with her, 'cause I love this woman and I feel what she feels. Two faces, one tear.

I don't know about her, but at that moment all the love in my heart went out to this woman, and I knew that with her was where I was meant to be. My love and honor and respect, and all the other feelings in between, were hers, and I was fine with that.

We held one another all night just talking and looking into each other's eyes. It felt real and not one time did I think of sex! I was content just sitting here with this woman and knowing that this had to be God telling me that this is and always has been your woman.

All the feelings that I had thought were gone came flooding back and knocked me on my ass. She woke me up in the wee hours and told me that she had to go home. We kissed and promised to talk again very soon. She thanked me and told me that she loved me. Then she was gone.

As I was leaving the complex, I felt I could eat something, so I went to Club Envy and paid to get in and get some chicken wings and fries. The club was closing and the young hoes that was running around half naked did not even phase me. I just wanted to eat my wings and take my ass home.

I didn't even remember going home, but I woke up in the bed next to my baby momma. She was trying to get into my phone!

Once she realized that I was awake, she put it down and said "I waited up for you all night, and as soon as I get to sleep you come up in here making all kinds of noise and shit, talking shit like you crazy, then passing out. I had to undress you and everything, Tyreque! You need to stop drinking that Remy V! The kids are gone to my grandmother's house and won't be back till Sunday night!"

I'm like do you want to do something? She says no, that she and her friend Mika was going to the casino, and did I want to go with them. I declined.

-------

I'm lying in bed watching Duke beat the shit out of UNC and I'm loving every minute of it. I hear my ring tone and it's my homeboy Mannie.

He like, "Damn Cuzzo, you just done forgot about me and C Boy, ain't you?"

"No, nigga, I just been ripping and running with this skateboard, shit. And I definitely got you and C Boy!"

Before I hang up with him, Mack calls and says that his sister's people are ready again, so I'm about to get my ass up. I ask him how many, and he says a starting line up like the show time Lakers. But I'm gone need a few minutes, and I'll call him back.

I hit Maria and ask her if Ricky is around, and she tells me yeah, and I tell her to tell him I'm ready. She tells me that the shit he left is still over her house. I tell her, "Okay, ten minutes and I'll be through there to get them."

--------

It's been a nice little minute since I saw Maria. She's like a real down ass bitch, and I feel like she got a lil' gangsta in her too.

I grab $40,000 out the stash and put it in my Gucci tote, then I jump into the shower and wash this ass. Fresh out of the shower, dressed and smelling like Polo Blue, I'm in the old school headed to see Maria.

I call Mack on the way and tell him to meet me at the spot in twenty-five minutes. When I pull up to Maria's house, she comes outside to greet me, and I instantly have flash backs of our little time together. I try to hand her the bag with the money in it but she tells me don't worry, this is another gift!

I follow her into the house and I'm like damn Maria, it looks like yo ass done got fatter since the last time I saw you.

"Yeah, I've been doing squats and trying to take care of my body. When can I see you again, baby?"

I'm like, *whenever you want to.* I'm thinking *you just gave me ten pounds of ice for free!*

I get the work and she sneaks in a kiss and I'm heading to the spot on Bishop to put this work up and wait on my play!

Mack gets there and he got the money and he riding solo dolo, so you know I like that! He takes the five and hands me $50,000, and out the door he goes! So, I got eight pounds of ice here and eight and a half pounds of cush and $90,000.

I never leave the money and the work at the same spot, so I got to make another trip to the house. As I'm walking out the door, Malcolm calls and say his lil dude is ready for that ten he said he was gone get, and that he is on his way to the spot. I go on and wait. It saved me another trip.

I tell him all I got right now is the eight and a half. He says cool, but he wants the other two as soon as I get them. I tell him, "Bet."

They get to the spot 15 minutes later and the play is made, so now I got like $118,900, and you know I'm going home to put that shit up.

Now I got to go back to Maria for the cush. Today has been a good day and I ain't been out but a few hours.

When I get to the house, it's cold as hell in this bitch and everyone is gone, so I open the safe and put the money inside. I'm doing the math real fast, and I come up with a ballpark figure of $249,500. It feels good to be able to do what you want when you want, but I know I can't live like this forever. But shit, right now I'm on a straight paper chase, and I can't stop. This shit is going too good.

I call Maria back and tell her that I'm going to need to get right on the green side, and she just laughs and says, "I was waiting for you to say that. Uncle Ricky said I can call him any time I need to."

But I'm like, "Look baby, I appreciate you for fucking with me but I'm bringing cash this time!"

She tells me, "Papi, I bought that shit for you and don't worry. You will pay me back one day, so are you coming or what?"

I tell her that it will be later, so I jump back into the old school and just ride. I'm on the freeway and I'm thinking it's about time to call my coded phone. It's been over 90 days since my last U.A. test.

The way that it works is, I call Saturday to see if I have to go Monday, so while I don't have shit going on, I punch in the number and listen to the extra bullshit until I hear my color code being called out for Monday. I just be having these lil feelings that lets me know to stay on point.

So now that I know that I have to go piss Monday, I have to start drinking water, even though I haven't started smoking and all that other shit. I have still been handling all kinds of shit.

I'm coming down Wright Avenue and I stop at the liquor store at the corner, right across the street from Baptist Car Wash. I'm straight with the dudes that own the liquor store. I fall in and speak to JR behind the counter.

"What up, Tyreque? Good to see you today. I been having problems with them kids hanging on the lot all day."

"Okay, JR. I got you baby. I'll have a talk with them on my way out."

"Okay. Thank you, Truth. I ain't trying to get nobody fucked up or nothing, it's just bad for business you know?"

"Of course, say no more. I got you, my man!"

"Thank you! What can I help you with? Remy V and Newports?"

"My man you already know how your dude rock. Add one tall cup of ice and a Sprite to that."

I come out and see a few dudes on the parking lot in they old schools. I know that they really don't mean no harm, but customers will keep going if they see them, 'cause they get tired of them asking for change and what not.

So, I say, "Hey y'all come over here. All this hanging on the lot is causing my people to lose business, so this is what we are going to do. Go in, get you a drink and get off this lot, okay?"

I hand each one of them a twenty. Then I pull across the street to the car wash and mix my drink up. Old School Hollywood asks can he wash my car, so I give him ten and pull into the stall and let him do his thing.

While he's washing the car, I'm on the phone with my cousin James, trying to see if he has something going on with his gambling spot tonight. He getting ready to go out of town, so the spot was closed. Then I hear my name being called from a car that was passing by. It looked like whoever it was is bending a block, so I was trying to get close to my car and that thing I got in the stash spot that I had buried.

But when the car pulls up, it's Lil Trice fine ass. I'm like, damn this lil bitch is bad, but for some reason, we didn't keep on fucking around in the beginning.

She looking at me then she says, "Nigga, why haven't I heard from you?"

I'm like, "Shit I had lost my phone with all my contacts in it and shit. It's never personal baby!"

"Well, my number is 758-3645."

I play like I'm putting it into my phone and ask her how has she been.

"I been good. Just trying to better myself and survive out here in this cold ass world!"

"Ain't shit wrong with that!"

I tell her that I'll give her a call and maybe we can hook up again. She says, "That's a bet," and with that she jumps back into her car and smashes out. Nigga was looking hard 'cause I'm telling you this lil bitch is bad, real talk.

Wood is drying my shit off and putting a shine to my rims. I'm looking around at my old hood, and it feels good to be free. I get back into my car and head up Wright Ave and turn right on 23rd Street. I'm about to pull up at the park where it all started.

I have so many memories in this neighborhood, some good and some bad, but all in all, they made me the man that I am today. The park is deserted, so I keep on rolling. This Remy got me feeling good, and since I'm so close to my homeboy Ron house, I decide to stop by and see what he got going. When I pull up, I let my music ring the bell for me.

"Truth, what up my nigga?"

"Not shit bro. Just maxing and relaxing. What 'bout you, homie, how have things been going your way?"

"You know, the same ole same ole. It's a struggle every day. Gotta roll on!"

"Ain't no question, Crip. Bro, you said you was gone look out for me on the music."

"I know. I've been putting shit in motion trying to get ahead of the game. I need to go put my hands in play as we speak, Cuzzo. I need like two of them bitches right now and on Crip, I got them gone in two days."

"Ok cuz. I'm gone bring them back through here later. You know I fucks with you my dude and if I got it, you got it!"

"I know that's right. Say no more."

While we standing around chopping it up, one of his wife's friends comes in and almost falls, so I catch her and say, "Be careful beautiful!"

"Oh my god! Thank you. I would have hurt myself pretty bad huh?"

With that she walks into the back room where Cuzzo wife is, then we hear his wife say, "Truth, your first impression was a good one. She wants to speak with you."

We exchange numbers and shit and that's that on that! I tell Ron to hit me up later and smash out.

I'm kind of hungry, so I'm looking for somewhere to get something to eat. I make a quick stop at K Hall, on the corner of Wright Ave and Battery Street. It's been jumping ever since I was a kid. They got some good ass cheeseburgers up in that bitch, plus they got some fresh ass crab legs they be selling on the weekends! And that's what I want.

It's so many fine ass chicks up here trying to get them crab legs, it's like a win-win, you feel me? Seafood and pussy!

I gone and order my shit and walk across the street to Crip 6 and holla at my Arabs behind the glass. They already know what I want, and they some cool motherfuckers. The young one be trying to get me to come work at the store, but I be telling him this ain't what you want. I'll have this bitch jumping like a crack house in the '90s, real talk.

When I get back across the street a lil youngster walks up to me and says, "Truth, my momma told me to give you your order, and for you to come back next week."

"Thank you lil man. Tell your mom that I'll be here for the same thing, same time."

I give him a ten spot.

My home girl Pimp live down the street, so I pull up at her house and holla at her for few minutes, then I pull around to my spot on Bishop. Once inside, I sit down and smash open a few crab legs and start eating the meat out them hoes. Damn, them hoes good.

My phone rings and it's this lil bitch named Leesha. She a real dick eater. I'm talking about the best head a nigga ever had. She can take the dick standing and bent over!

V. P. Taylor

# (Trinity) Ball of Confusion

It's been three weeks since I've eaten anything close to a meal. I have probably lost a total of ten pounds just in these last few days. Who needs food when you're living off nothing but pure nerves and emotions?

I have to force myself to eat anything besides a cracker here or there. Oh! I just added a cube of cheese and an apple to the mix, so things are looking up. I know that I cannot go on in this state forever. You would've literally thought that I had run into a ghost. Well, if that is the case, I've been being hunted for the last three weeks.

The calls and texts did not stop coming, and I did not stop accepting them (that last part)!

*Trinity! What in the world are you doing?* I said to myself. *This isn't closure, this is hoe-sure.*

All I can think about is the man's body next to mine, his touch, his kiss, how hard he got in my hands, how he plucked my pussy like a guitar.

*Good Lord, please save me.*

Ok, so let me back up now and try to explain how Truth and I got from a night of heartfelt tears to scenes from 'Fifty Shades of Grey.'

That last 'I love you' text on that Sunday night should've sealed the deal, but for some reason it only reinforced mountains of thoughts and feelings that I had been pushing through. I can't believe that after all of these years, Truth still loves me! I can't believe after years of living as a robot, when it comes to my feelings, that I feel anything at all, let alone love.

*Where Lord? Where is this coming from?*

At the ripe old age of 33, I thought that I had put away childish things such as dolls, Disney movies and love (yuck). But nope. Here I am with a stomach full of butterflies for the past three weeks.

Anyway, back to the movie.

If you've ever watched TV and seen an ad for Lay's potato chips, you know the line about how you can't eat just one. I've never done research on it, but my personal experience has pretty much proven it to be true.

Truth became my favorite flavor of chips, and I could not get enough of him. And it wasn't just the calls and texts. I wanted to see him and be around him. To feel his energy and lie in his arms. But there is a price to pay for wanting what we should not have, and that price is addiction. I'm not sure if it was the fact that I had let myself meet him the first time, or if I had opened up a Pandora's Box of feelings and couldn't put them back in, or if it's just that Truth turned me on.

When I saw a text from him or heard his voice over the phone, something came alive in me, and my curiosity got the best of me. For a few days, hearing from him was good enough. But when I didn't hear from him, I would drive myself crazy with my thoughts.

*Does he really love me? I'm sure he doesn't want to break up his family or mine. But can't we just be friends? Why am I acting like this? Lord Help Me Please!*

As soon as those thoughts would overtake me, I'd get that text or that call from him.

"Hey, baby. I didn't want anything. Just calling to tell you that I love you and I'm thinking about you."

Oh, my gosh. All of my girlie thoughts and dreams and hopes that I had long abandoned would flood my soul.

I'm too much of an OG or chicken, whichever, to call him, so until he called me, I would just sit there and stew in my madness. When I wasn't actively driving myself insane with a million questions, I was driving myself insane with guilt.

I have a whole husband and not just a 'we met a few years ago' husband. A 'we've been together for two decades and have the three kiddos to prove it' kind of husband.

Although my marriage had not been the best (to put it mildly), I did take my vows and commitment seriously. It killed me to know that I could not put a stop to these ever-growing feelings for Truth.

It's like that game Whack-A-Mole. As soon as I thought I had stuffed this feeling down, it would pop back up. I'd go from ooey-gooey feelings to lust to guilt to sadness to anger all in the matter of minutes until I heard his voice again, and nothing else mattered in that moment.

So, when the calls and texts started to be about meeting up again, I was an emotional wreck.

--------

I had extra office space at work that I was renting to see my private clients, and on this particular night, I was the client that was in need. The building was empty. I had him meet me there around midnight.

I don't think I closed or locked the door good before I was all over him.

*Where the hell did this come from? And who is this woman that took over my body?*

I don't know if it was that he knew this moment was coming, because Truth has definitely been known to be a ladies' man, or if he was just as scared as I was, but whatever the case, he took full control of me.

He slowed me down and kissed me softly where my tongue caught his rhythm. It was the perfect kiss. He led me to one of my couches and the next thing I knew I was almost completely undressed.

I asked him did he have a condom and he told me that he didn't. At that point, passion had almost completely taken over me. I did not care.

His fingers were stroking my clit as I let out a soft purr. I felt heaven and earth move.

He took his time, gently kissing my lips and nibbling my neck, and then my breasts. I felt him through his pants and he was rock hard. I couldn't help but think, *all this just for me?*

I gently pulled down his jeans and boxers to reveal what I felt like I had been waiting for forever. I don't remember our lovemaking when we were young, but I do remember how I felt in that moment - like I was fourteen, and was underneath him for the first time, and that this was all I ever wanted in my life.

Just as he is getting ready to enter me and feel just how much I've missed him; he stopped and turned me to look him in his eyes.

"Trinity, baby, are you sure?"

I don't know if it was the sincerity in his eyes that stopped me or what, but I was halted in space and time. On one hand, I didn't care about anything other than feeling his hard dick in the softest parts of me, but on the other hand, I didn't know what this would mean for us.

There's always been something about the way he looks and speaks to me. I can tell just about anything with him by those two things. It wasn't *that* he asked me if I was sure. It was *how* he asked.

If you've never believed in such a thing as soulmates, then this may be the point where you stop reading. I had never been much of a believer in the idea myself. I believed in a simpler way of thinking: you choose who you mate, and you choose whether to stick it out or leave.

With Truth I have no choice. I'm a slave to those eyes and the way that he looks at me and the way he speaks to me. Just one word from him can change the whole course of my thoughts. And that's what happened that night.

Hearing him ask me, in the sincerest way, if I was sure, resonated in my soul.

*Was I sure?*

To be completely honest, I hadn't been sure of anything in the last three weeks; whether I was coming or going, or if my head was attached to my body.

My pussy was throbbing, but my heart pounded louder than I had ever experienced before, because I knew that if we allowed our bodies to do this dance, it could mean the end of the life that I knew before.

It wasn't until several months later that that dance became the hammer to the nail of both our coffins.

V. P. Taylor

## (Trinity) Bag of Bullshit

What do you do with someone that you love, and who loves you, when you decide not to fuck? After our late-night rendezvous that ended with me having the female version of blue balls, we continued to talk and stay in touch.

I felt awkward, like I had a third breast or something, because I'd never had a man that had the opportunity to feel my pleasure and didn't take full advantage. It takes a lot for me to even get to that point with any man, because my mother raised such a lady (yeah, right).

But no, it's because of the whole demisexual nature. While I have seen many handsome guys in my time, my little girl only gets wet for the man that I'm connected to. That's great for the guy in my life, but kind of sucks for my inner hoe.

So, here I am in love up to my eyeballs and sexually frustrated as hell because the man that I really want is more interested in being my friend than my lover, or so I thought.

I just wasn't used to this type of affection from a man. Most of my other relationships, as long or as short as they existed, were very sexual in nature. I mean, once the connection is there, I like to connect and connect and connect some more. You get it. So, for me to spend time with Truth, as deeply as our physical connection was, I couldn't understand why there was no sex involved.

We would go for rides in the car during the middle of the night and talk for hours about everything, although we tried to stay away from too many conversations about our home life or significant others. I had never had an affair during my marriage, and although I knew that spending so much time with Truth was wrong, my emotions were like a roller coaster. If a person wants to understand what an emotional affair looks like, this was it.

We would hold hands, and kiss from time to time, but neither one of us would ever let it go farther than that. Although I craved him so much, he would always reassure me that he wasn't with me for sex, and that he just wanted to spend time with me.

For most women, this would be sweet, and it's not that it wasn't, it's just that it made me even more confused.

--------

I started to wonder what the purpose in all of this was if we were not going to be together. Why would we risk our relationships at home just to spend time together?

I figured that he had other irons in the fire. And after spending so much time together, he opened up and shared a lot with me about his doggish ways with his son's mother and with other women in his life. But the more he opened up and shared with me, the more confused I became.

I had been used to my husband constantly lying to me about major and minor things. To have Truth being true to his name floored me.

I mean, why would a guy who's interested in me tell me so many things about himself that could possibly alter the way that I felt about him? If he was a gambling man, the bet to place his heart and his truth in my hands paid off.

Not only did it not change the way I viewed him, instead, his honesty made me respect him more. He was slowly becoming my best friend and I began to try to make sense of this thing between us. Truth wasn't making any promises to me, nor was he asking for us to be together. I felt like I was in a suspended state, somewhere between pure bliss and sheer anxiety.

--------

I had managed to keep my growing affection for Truth away from my husband. He was hardly ever at home anyway, and when he was he only wanted one thing from me and it wasn't conversation or to hold my hand. I found myself trying to fuck my way through my feelings.

I calculated that if I engaged my husband and put in more time, effort and energy into our relationship, with sex in the mix, I'd get over my infatuation with Truth. As he opened up to me more and more, thoughts and hopes of our being involved again diminished.

When I had first started back talking with him, he had told me that he was about 70% ready to change and become a better man, but there was 30% that was still involved in the streets. As we spent more time together the realities of that 30% could not be denied.

I loved the fact that he never tried to hide himself or his life from me, but I can't lie, thoughts of why it didn't work for us in the past began to resurface. I was filled with so many mixed emotions, and I wasn't sure if they were coming from my husband or from Truth.

My husband had treated me poorly for years, but he was always there, always constant, always dependable. Even though things were rocky for us, we had just kind of settled into the dysfunction of our relationship. I probably could've gone on like that with my husband for another twenty years but reconnecting with Truth had me longing for more.

At a minimum, it made me want to cling to what I currently had with Truth, even if there was no sex or security involved. For many women this would have been a perfect situation. I have one man who provides stability, security, and sex, and I have my other man who provides me with love and comfort and companionship.

By any stretch of the imagination, I wasn't lacking for anything. But this was not only a ball of emotions, but also a bag of bullshit, because I was frustrating myself going between two men to try to piece together all of my needs.

Call me old fashioned (I'm sure that I am), but I've always wanted one man to provide all of my needs. I know that it's unrealistic to think that one person can fulfill all of your needs, but I always felt that I wasn't that needy a chick. I don't need to be wined and dined I just needed the basics - love, companionship, support, security, connection and commitment.

*Is that too much to ask?*

Whereas Truth had my first three covered, my husband had always been responsible for covering those last three (loosely). I found myself becoming more and more frustrated, because I felt that I needed to make a decision, but in reality, there was no decision to be made. Truth had never asked anything of me, and I wasn't asking him to leave his family to be with me.

I had a bag of bullshit among my baggage, and the feeling of being stuck with a life full of shit. Good shit, bad shit. But you have no clue what to do with any of it.

# (Trinity) Bankruptcy

Have you ever just been mentally, physically and spiritually drained? Well, I have.

This, my friends, is why I was so against love from the beginning. I'm an extremely passionate person, so I tend to give my all to whatever it is that I am involved in. I think that makes me excellent in a lot of ways, because I'm a giver, and if I give you my all, it's certainly a blessing. But sometimes for me, on the giving end leaves me depleted.

I'm tired, I have nothing left to give. I'm bankrupt!

When love is your gift to give, and you've given it as much as you can with no real changes or rewards or benefits, it makes you feel hopeless. That's how I began to feel.

This once vibrant and bubbly therapist was in need of therapy herself.

I felt like Truth was dangling me on a string. He had me right where he wanted me, but for some reason he would not close the deal.

Tony had left me by the wayside years ago, but he eventually sniffed around and found remnants of Truth left on me.

It had been about three months since Truth and I had been back in touch with each other and, even though I knew that my feelings for him were deep, we had not really progressed past the friendship phase. In my mind I began to believe that we were friends.

I had to put my relationship with him somewhere, in some category, because it was driving me crazy to be in constant suspense. I had told him that he wasn't ready for anything with me and that I didn't want to force him, but I didn't want to lose him either, so I would be content with his friendship.

Wrong.

So, one day Tony and I were in the car when Truth called me and I answered the phone (I know crazy, right?), but we were just friends! When I told my husband who I had been talking to, he hit the roof. He cursed me from here to Japan and back. I couldn't get a single word in.

My relationship with Truth was so gentle and so open and transparent that for one second, I forgot that my marriage was not!

In my mind I had convinced myself that because Truth and I weren't having sex, I wasn't cheating. I hadn't shared with my husband any of our kissing, holding hands, or hours spent in each other's company, but I did tell him that we had been back in contact for the last few months, and that I was trying to help him get back on his feet after being away for so long.

I told him that Truth was in a relationship, and that he had been a perfect gentleman with me, and compared to the way I was with him, that was generally accurate.

Although it shouldn't have surprised me that Tony reacted that way, it really caught me off guard. I really felt that Tony didn't care what I did or was doing as long as I wasn't sleeping with anyone else, and for all intents and purposes, I wasn't.

But boy was I wrong. He cared big time, and my ass was feeling the burn.

Tony had never been physically abusive towards me. Well, I should say that he hadn't yet, but that's for another part of the story. Although he hadn't been physically abusive, he was verbally, emotionally, and mentally abusive. He was very controlling, and I think because of the type of woman I am - being more involved in my career than socially - I made it pretty easy for him to control me.

I've pretty much had the same group of friends since either childhood or early adulthood, and up to this point, outside of church and work, I really don't do much.

It wasn't really because of anything that he had done or not done. It's just that I'm pretty easy like Sunday morning. The only reason that I had so much time on my hands to spend with Truth, either on the phone or late-night meet ups, was because my husband was always gone.

Tony works every day, but he is also about thirty percent still in the streets as well. His street activity typically involved gambling and dice, and the things that go along with that lifestyle. I have always been against it, but through the years, I had just grown weary of fighting and more comfortable with him being gone.

I didn't complain when thousands of dollars were being added to my accounts, or when the kids and I could do shopping sprees out of the blue, so I had learned to accept some of the compromises of the lifestyle as well. Those compromises could include him losing money and me having to cover extra bills in the household. Sometimes they would include women who hung out to try to catch a baller, and most times they would include me going to bed alone and waking up alone most nights, especially on weekends.

Now this is not the part of the story where I want people to feel sorry for me, or to justify what I have done up to this point. I'm just simply explaining how I had so much free time.

Needless to say, once one dog catches the scent of another in his yard, the defenses go up. Part of Tony's control over me is the way he wears me down with question after question, until he is satisfied. I can't stand tension or feeling anxious, so if he keeps battering me with those things, it's likely I will cave.

I'm not the best liar, and it's because I just don't like the anxiety that goes with having to keep it up. In a lot of ways, I felt lighter now that the cat was out the bag at this point.

I didn't quite understand what was happening between Truth and me and had nothing to lie about. I was lost myself, so what I could share with my husband was pretty much all that I had, minus a few details.

We weren't dating, and outside of a few phone calls and texts between us, we weren't spending that much time together. When I would talk to Truth, he seemed more and more preoccupied with the issues in his life. He would share his thoughts and feelings with me, but generally skipped the details about what all he had going on.

I had just resigned that I would be a support to him when he needed it and that was it. After things died down with Tony and me, I tried to salvage some sense of normalcy in my life.

Little did I know how far from normal I had become.

# (Trinity) This House is Not a Home

As I tried to get my life back to normal again, normal didn't feel good anymore. Once Tony was assured that Truth wasn't peeing on any of his trees, he went back to his life as usual. The late-night calls and conversations with Truth had died down somewhat, and our talks became briefer and occasional.

I would still often think of him but would be too afraid to reach out to him. As the time and distance between us grew, I became more and more shy and awkward with him. I believe it was partly due to him becoming more shy and awkward with me.

Sometimes he would call me just to say hello, or just to hear my voice, but that would be it. One night he called me just to tell me that he loved me and that he wanted to be loved. When I told him that I loved him, he told me that he knew and that he would call me later.

His conversation became rather cryptic (no pun intended), and he wasn't willing to tell me all he had going on. I didn't have the nerve to ask.

With Tony back to his usual self, and Truth seemingly avoiding contact with me, I was back down to just me, and boy, was that a lonely place to be.

I had never really realized how lonely I was until that time. It's like Truth came back into my life and filled me up with everything that I had been missing, that I didn't even know I was missing.

But when he pulled back, it didn't leave me empty in the way I was before. It left me emptier, because now I remembered what it felt like to be full. One of my favorite sayings in therapy is 'once you know something, there is no such thing as unknowing it.'

Now that I know these things are missing, I can either do something about it or not, but I can't not know it.

But honestly, after months of emotional gymnastics, I was too tired and exhausted to even try to figure out what to do. I had suggested counseling or therapy for Tony and me, but he refused, so I began seeing a therapist by myself.

--------

By this time, I had enlisted the help of several of my closest friends, including my two besties from childhood who had lived through my adolescent Truth days. But I found myself still not feeling settled or peaceful regarding all that had happened. My house was still my house, but it was not my home.

If home is where the heart is, then my home was with Truth, and I didn't know how to get evicted.

I could not get past my feelings for this man. At this point I wasn't even concerned about how he had felt about me, because it was my feelings that I was having to wrestle with, not his.

Looking back on all of this now, I'm so grateful I didn't have to contend with his feelings as well, because when his feelings did eventually show up, that was a whole other ball of wax.

I digress.

Because I'm such an emotionless woman, I didn't know what to do with my girl feelings, so I did what any good, southern, Christian woman would do: I drank them away, or at least tried to.

I've never been a big drinker, and as a matter of fact, I only have one drink that I like, and that's Crown and Coke, or if I'm being cheap, Seagram's Seven and Coke. I've also tried them both with Sprite, which we call a Dirty Sprite, but that's neither here nor there.

So, the following winter, after this life-altering reconnection, I tried to drown my sorrows in the bottle. It would probably take me a month to finish a fifth of Crown, but for me to drink alone was a new thing.

Here it is right before Christmas, and of course Christmas is the time for holiday spirits, yet I'm declining before my own eyes. I had done well with not calling Truth and just being a caring friend when he called. I was getting back on track at home, but the nagging on the inside would not go away.

I was at a Christmas party one night and had probably had a little more to drink than I was used to, so I called Truth to see what he was doing. To my surprise he wasn't busy and wanted to see me.

He left his car on the block, and I picked him up and we headed to a friend's house. As soon as I got him in the door, I was all over him - kissing him, straddling him - all while my friend was watching TV on the other couch.

*What had gotten into me?*

I had done so well at holding myself together. By this time in our 'situation-ship', we were comfortable just being friends.

*Was I just so very desperate for that connection that the alcohol gave me the courage I needed to go for it?*

Whatever the case, the night was interrupted by a phone call from my husband, asking where I was. Then I caught a glimpse of what looked to be him rolling through the parking lot. That'll make you sober up right quick.

After that night, I told myself that I would have to get myself under control, commit to figuring out what was missing in my life, and discover why I kept turning to Truth to find it.

To throw myself at someone like I did - someone who clearly only wants to be a friend to me - was pathetic and a new all-time low for me. I made a resolution to stop pining over a man who doesn't want me, and to make use of what the Lord has given me, even if I wasn't necessarily happy with how everything had turned out.

It had been right at a year since I saw Truth in that restaurant that day, and I had almost completely changed from the woman that I knew so well before.

On the cusp of a new year, and hopefully a whole new me, I was unsuspecting of what lay ahead.

I was destined for some changes.

## (Trinity) Baby It's Cold Outside

Of the top five things that contribute to a depressed mood, winter is definitely near the top. If you know anything about Arkansas weather, you know that it doesn't typically adhere to a calendar of seasons. In other words, Arkansas doesn't give a damn what season it is. It does what it wants to.

But this year, after a string of mild winters, winter came in with a full vengeance. In Arkansas, just a light dusting of snow on the road shuts the city down. This year, there was a full ice storm. I mean, people's lights were out for days, and there were street crews working around the clock. This winter was a real son of a bitch.

I had suffered not only a 'Love TKO' this year, but to top it all off, I couldn't even find a decent distraction, what with all of the horrible weather. I was stuck at home to mope around and drink my sorrows away.

Out of nowhere, my phone goes off, and it's him.

I hadn't heard from him since I damn near jumped his bones after that party. I knew that my husband and kids were at home. Hell, everyone's family was at home due to the city shutting down, but I didn't care.

"Hello, Trinity?"

"Yes, this is she…"

"This is Truth. I was just calling to check on you and see if you were okay, with the ice storm and all."

I told him that I was.

"Trinity, I really love you, and I miss you."

I melted, and I told him that I missed him to.

He asked me where my husband was, and I told him that he was asleep. He asked me if I needed to get off the phone and I told him no.

We talked for about an hour (I know, risky), but it's like, as much as I tell myself that we're just friends, and that I'm going to be okay - when I hear his voice, I melt.

We talked about his reasons for not pursing a sexual relationship, and he shared with me that he doesn't want to hurt me with everything that he has going on in his life. He shared with me how it felt to lose me all those years ago, and that he couldn't take that type of pain again. Rather than begin something with me while he knows that he is not ready, he would rather that we just continue to be friends.

I tell him that I respect that, but I can't help but feel like I am being placed on hold.

It's at moments like this when I have to slap myself into reality. I have a husband asleep in the next room. Even if I don't like it, I know that Tyreque is telling me the truth.

Hearing this man declare his love, thoughts and feelings towards me makes it better, but it also makes it worse. I don't think that he really understands what all of this is doing to me and has done to me over the course of the past year.

*How can someone break your heart and kiss it at the same time?*

That's how I feel, because even though I don't want to hear the truth, I need to.

He tells me that he has been fighting with himself and his feelings for me, knowing that I am another man's wife.

"Trinity, I have never messed with anyone else's wife."

I tell him that I understand, and I do, but then it makes me angry because why continue to reach out to me?

He tells me it's because he needs to hear my voice, and that he needs to know if I am okay, but I feel like those are selfish reasons. If you know that we cannot do this, then why keep it going?

In my heart I know that I need to stop doing this to myself, and with the New Year coming in, I am going to do just that.

--------

Thirty days and no Truth.

I blocked his number from my phone so that I wouldn't even know if he was calling me or not. 'Out of sight, out of mind' has always been a useful truth for me.

Besides, I was able to let him go as a fourteen-year-old girl. Surely as a thirty-four-year-old grown ass, boss woman such as myself I can do the same.

It was one of the toughest things I had ever done in my life, but I knew that I had to do it for my sanity. If Truth couldn't do it for himself, I could do it for me. Besides, it was only satisfying him to hear my voice. I needed and felt that I deserved more.

I'm not sure why I felt that way. We were not together as a couple and hadn't been since junior high school. But for whatever reason, I felt that he was mine, and that if I couldn't have him in the way that I wanted him, he couldn't have me at all.

I know that I was being a bit of a baby, and a bit extreme, but I was tired of Truth playing with my feelings, and I was tired of jockeying with them myself. I wondered if he even tried to call, if he might've thought that something was wrong with my phone, or if he even cared.

--------

On day thirty-one, I got a call from his little cousin, telling me that Truth had gotten into trouble and was possibly heading back to prison. I felt ten million waves of emotions all at once. But the most compelling one was the feeling of having been stupid. How selfish of me to shut myself off from him like I had, and for no other reason than I couldn't control my feelings for him.

*What type of friend was I being?*

If it wasn't my way, then it was the highway? I didn't feel that way when I originally closed myself off from him. I had felt like I was doing it for the both of us. For him and for me. I didn't want to pressure him to do anything he was uncomfortable with (messing with a married woman), or anything that he wasn't ready for (leaving the streets, or being in a faithful, committed relationship).

So, rather than secretly wanting things from him that he couldn't give, and that I didn't need, I decided that stepping back was best and safest place for me.

But at this point, none of that mattered. All that I was concerned about was my friend's situation.

I immediately unblocked his number, and I called him. He explained to me that he was okay, and that his cheating and playboy ways had caught up with him and led to a domestic disturbance between him and his son's mother. Although she had put her hands on him and he had not fought her back, the incident put him in a negative light with his probation officer and the judge.

I didn't know that things were that bad for him at home, or if any of the risks he was taking were on my account. He told me that he had violated his probation, and that the judge may send him to a halfway house, as opposed to federal prison, to finish out the remainder of his sentence.

He explained to me that although it was bullshit, he was willing to deal with the consequences, however they played out. I told him that if he needed me, I was here for him.

We never discussed my blocking him from my phone.

---------

A week later I get a call from Truth.

"Hey Trinity."

"Yes."

"Baby, I need to be with you tonight. Can you get away?"

Tony is back to his old ways, so I'm probably alone at least until 4 or 5 am. I tell him yes, that I can see him.

"Trinity, one more thing. Are you ready for me to make love to you tonight?"

After months and months of what I considered to be a game of cat and mouse, and after months and months of him holding me at bay, and after our conversation during the ice storm when he explained to me why he was hesitant to take our relationship there, he asks me this? Now, facing the possibility of him going back to prison, I am speechless.

"Trinity are you there?"

"Yes, Truth I'm here."

"Did you hear me baby?"

"I heard you, and yes, I'm ready."

--------

As I hang up the phone, I don't feel anything. I don't feel nervous, I don't feel excited, I don't feel anything.

Now, after all these months of constantly dealing with my feelings, I get to this moment and I got nothing. No butterflies, no warm and ooey gooey feeling, no nothing. At this point, I realize that I have got to be the craziest person alive.

*Thirty days ago, you were done with Truth, and wanted off of this rollercoaster of emotional torment, and now you're prepared to ride his dick. Trinity, you have had ten months to think through the ramifications of this. He has saved you from yourself, and probably himself too, at least twice before, and you are still going to do this? Girl, you crazy!*

I'm talking to myself because there is no one else to call to tell this bullshit to. Yes, I wanted to feel him inside of me ten months ago, and yes, I still do today. Nothing else mattered.

My answer was yes.

So, here's where the story gets more bizarre.

Whatever courage it took for him to make that call had obviously vanished, because from that point forward, I had to take the lead. Outside of him paying for the hotel room, you would've thought that Truth was a virgin, and I was coming to pop his cherry.

He was stuttering and stammering when I called him back to let him know that I was ready to meet.

When we finally met up, later that evening, he was pussy footing around. I don't remember Truth ever being this shy, but this wasn't the most bizarre place we had been in, so I ignored all of the signs of hesitation on his part. It was time for him to put his money where his mouth was, so to speak.

--------

It started out slowly. We got to the room, and he wanted to talk. I kissed him and undid his belt and his pants. The lights were completely off, and I dropped down to my knees to find that his dick was completely hard before I even put him in my mouth.

Yeah, little Truth was ready even if big Truth was not.

I sucked his dick and licked his balls like I had waited my whole life to do so. I heard him let out the softest moan, which gave me the green light to keep going. He stopped me and pulled me up to meet his mouth and gave me the most gentle kiss. Then he undressed me.

He laid me on the bed and kissed my pearl tongue. He kissed and licked her until I was dizzy.

This was the farthest we had come since this friendship thing first began, and I was as anxious as a child is on Christmas day. I was so ready that the spot where I had been sitting was soaking wet.

He came up for air and looked me in the eyes. He told me he loved me as he put his hard dick between my soft and open thighs. As soon as his dick spread my lips and I felt him inside of me, it was like my every wish had come true.

He let out a moan as I let out my purr, and we both came alive. He started out on top of me, taking this pussy all in as he stared into my eyes. I reached up to kiss him, because I couldn't handle the intensity of his gaze as he made love to my soul and my body.

My tongue was going in and out of his mouth as my wet pussy was gripping his hard dick. He had to slow down, or it would've meant a complete eruption from both of us.

He got up and turned me over, with me on my knees and my ass in the air. I know that every girl is not a fan of doggy-style, but penetration from behind is my weakness, and Truth knew how to make me weak.

He took every piece of me, as I offered him everything that I had to give. Our moans grew louder and stronger with every thrust, until finally we exploded together. The moment after we came, I did not want to let this man go. I wanted to continue touching him and to be near him.

I was completely naked, as was he, and I didn't even know where to begin to look. I started to get my clothes together to go home, but I could not move. I felt so welcome and warm being up under Truth. He was my fire, and I wasn't going back into the icy air without him.

We talked and held hands and lay in each other's arms into the morning. I even saw Truth's eyes well up with tears during one of our talks. It had to be about eight in the morning when my phone rang and woke me from my peaceful sleep. It was my husband.

--------

The sound of my phone woke Truth up. He had cut both of his phones off well into the night, but I explained to him that I had kids and that I couldn't, and he understood.

I told Tony a lie that I knew that he wouldn't believe, but he had to get to work, so I knew he wouldn't keep me on the phone for long. I would deal with whatever trouble awaited me when I got home later that day.

Truth asked me if I had to go, and I told him no, that I wasn't through with him yet. I got up and dressed myself. I needed to run to the store to get a few personal things. When I returned, Truth had made coffee and gotten us breakfast from the hotel lobby.

I smiled as I thought to myself 'nice touch,' but we wouldn't be doing any eating this morning. My appetite was not for food. I tried to nibble on it just to let him know that I appreciated his efforts.

When I finished nibbling, he wanted me to lie in his arms as he searched the TV for a movie to watch. I lay in his arms as if this is what we always did after a night filled with passion. We talked, like we always did these last few months, about our lives and the various things that we were going through.

If I hadn't ever valued it before, in this moment, I valued the friendship between Truth and me. Nothing was forced, the conversation was easy and honest, and when he mentioned how my pussy felt like velvet, and how good and wet it was, I knew it was time for round two and three and four.

I think I made him tap out, but that's what he got for making me wait so long.

V. P. Taylor

# The Aftermath

# (Trinity) So Why Do You Stay

I came into that relationship thinking that it was perfect. That he was perfect. I put my all into an attempt to establish what I thought would be the perfect life. I was young, and although I thought that I was up on game, I was still very naive when it came to love and relationships.

I allowed Tony to kind of break me down, and became a needy, dependent woman. I had never been that before. I had always been pretty secure within myself, and I pretty much did my own thing. I was never afraid to go against the grain or be alone.

That changed over the course of my years with Tony. I began to feel like I needed him and couldn't live without him. Even now, as I type, I still have the fear that I can't do it without him, and it's crazy, because I know I can. Perhaps somewhere along the way, I just got tired of trying. His dominance in the relationship kept me thinking that I couldn't be without him.

I would fight it and buck the system, but I would never leave him, no matter how crazy or disrespectful things got. Out of the twenty-plus years that we've been together, I only left once, and that was when I was pregnant with our oldest daughter.

I was sixteen years old and pregnant, and I'd found out that he was cheating on me with some broad who was buying him things and giving him money. I was about five months pregnant, and once I found out, it was a wrap for me immediately. There was no way that I was going to stay with a nigga so low down that he would cheat on me while I was carrying his child.

I mean, I left his ass without a second thought, and although it hurt, I had still had a few guys on the bench who were just waiting to get in the game. As I said before, I wasn't ever really faithful, especially after I saw that Tony wasn't either. I felt like 'what's good for the goose is certainly good for the gander.'

By the time I got pregnant and actually decided to have the child, we were about two years in, and accustomed to drama and infidelity. I had a couple of male friends but had only slept with one other guy during that time period. He was twenty-two and I was sixteen, and I had no business fucking him, but he was cool. We were cool, and at that time, I just needed someone off the radar.

His name was Julius, and I was not physically attracted to him at all. He was light skinned, with grey eyes. I prefer my men dark skinned. He was kind of thuggish, which I liked back then, because I've always felt like I would run smooth over a 'good' guy. He could handle my little tough ass, but the main reason that I really liked Julius, outside of the fact that he was someone totally different, was that he was an intellectual.

He had a few college hours behind him and had attended Philander. He was smart and he was cool and he was a hustler. We spent a lot of time together smoking (cause by this time I was smoking weed on a regular basis) and philosophizing.

One of the factors that led me to fool with him was that he had been there for me when my grandmother passed away. I met him the summer before starting the eleventh grade, while I was working at Andy's, and he approached me and asked me for my number.

At the time, Tony was doing his thang, and I guess I had fallen off my job, which was keeping him completely occupied and drained, because by the end of tenth grade, I had several hoes calling me, asking about our relationship.

I knew he was just doing him, and I wasn't really bothered, because I was always taking applications as well. So, when Julius came along, it just so happened that I had an open spot on the team.

We were cool just kicking it, no sex, just hanging out. I'm a guy's girl, so I like guy shit; sports, talking shit, playing cards, drinking, smoking, and all that. I'm a daddy's girl. I could be around a man 24/7, and never be bored.

On the flip side, women annoy the fuck out of me, and I'll never understand how they can talk nonstop about hair and makeup, or whine about how men do this and that. I'm like Biggie: *soon as he buy that wine, I just creep up from behind.*

Hell. While y'all women complaining, I'm swooping up the boys and adding them to my team.

I love men and they tend to love me, and Julius was no exception. We enjoyed being around each other. We would ride and smoke and drink and talk bullshit. It was cool. During that time of chilling with him, my grandmother passed away, and I was devastated.

The craziest thing is, that Tony was nowhere to be found during that time. Like, the entire week of planning the funeral, he was MIA, and he and my grandmother had been cool. Julius had never met her before, but he was there for me and my mom.

I know you all are wondering why my mother allowed her sixteen-year-old daughter to date a twenty-two-year-old man. It's simple. She liked him.

He talked with my mom about grown up shit, and he was respectful towards my parents. If they told him to have my ass home at midnight, I was home on time. Sometimes we were just sitting outside the house. He was respectful, and he talked shit that my momma liked, so they were cool.

After a few months of friendship, and seeing what type of guy he was, I grew to feel connected with him enough to sleep with him. And that was the beginning of the end of our relationship, for me.

Now, I'm not that damned experienced with sex, but that shit was whack. Again, I'm very sexual and my relationship with Tony was almost purely physical (fighting and fucking), so there was no way that I could have anything serious with someone I did not enjoy fucking.

I may have slept with him a total of five times throughout our entire relationship and can only remember one time that I enjoyed it, and that was probably because he was so into it, I got his ass to screaming. If his sex game had been better, maybe we could have had something.

But as soon as I gave him some, he became possessive.

I remember one day we went to the mall, and I saw a childhood guy friend, and stopped to talk. Julius' crazy ass just walked off, and then he turned around and looked at me like, *bitch, come on.* Prior to this episode, he had never been aggressive or abusive to me, but after this happened, things changed.

In order to prevent any issues between this childhood friend and my half-nigga (because remember, at this point he really ain't my nigga, like that), I said my goodbyes and walked away. Once he saw me walking, he started walking again, like, ten steps ahead of me. We were heading towards the escalator, and as soon as he was down far enough to where he couldn't come back up, I ducked off on his ass.

I can imagine how stupid he must've felt when he turned around and I wasn't there.

Although I rode to the mall with him, I am never afraid to bounce on anyone or any situation that I don't feel comfortable in. I got a ride to the house from my brother.

I had ever seen that man so damn mad at me. He blew my little pager the fuck up, but I was unbothered until the next morning. Bright and early, before I left for school and after my parents had left the house, he showed up. That little muthafucker jacked my ass up outside of my house and I promise I saw his grey eyes turn red.

That was the only incident we had, but that was enough to let me know that he was no less controlling than Tony, and without the benefits. After that, he would still take me to school sometimes, and pick me up if I needed it, but that was pretty much it.

I remember that after I had my daughter, he would still come around to see me and do little things for me, but I had to cut him loose because it was going nowhere. You have to be able to fuck me right, at a minimum, and I know that's shallow, but it is what it is.

It was shortly after that relationship ended that I got pregnant for the second time. But this time, we decided to have the baby.

--------

So, back on track. About a month before I had my daughter, we decided to give it another shot. Being a single mother was not something that I wanted for myself, so I was all about trying to make it work.

We did get it back on track for a while. We had a few bumps and bruises along the way, but for the most part, I just gave up on having a life outside of him and gave in to just being his ride.

For the next few years, I had no life outside of Tony, even on the night of my graduation. I didn't go out with my friends. I was with him. Whenever he would go to the different little gambling spots, I was in there with him, or waiting in the car.

I worked a little off and on, and after graduation I went to college, but that was basically it. I became a member of the church that his family belonged to. Outside of Jewells, I didn't have any other friends outside of his family and friends. I basically disappeared into him, and he loved it. In exchange for my personal freedom, he gave me his undying devotion again, until.....

V. P. Taylor

# (Trinity) My World Came to an End

One day I woke up, and my day began with having a mother, and by lunch time, I didn't. She was gone.

My relationship with her was strained for most of my adolescence. We loved each other, but a lot of the time, I felt that I was not the daughter that she had hoped to have. We were polar opposites, with the primary difference being that she valued stability and security, and I valued riding with no hands. I felt like I scared my momma to death, figuratively, but during my periods of depression following her death, I felt that was literally so.

She was such a cautious person, and I have always been a risk taker who throws caution to the wind. We loved each other - I know this for sure - but we were so different. Unfortunately, I didn't come with a user manual, so my momma really didn't know what to do with me.

Our dynamic was a little stressful when I was a child, but it became catastrophic as I entered my teenage years. We had some real knock-down, drag-outs, and unfortunately, I never got the opportunity to have my momma as a friend. I would like to believe that we would've eventually gotten there, because, as I began to understand myself better, I would have tried to help her understand me. But life happened, and that dream never became a reality.

After I had my daughter, my relationship with my mother did improve some, largely due to the fact that having a child just settled me down some, but also because now my mother's focus was off of trying to protect me, and onto protecting her grandchild.

My baby made my momma so happy. It's crazy, because something as negative as being a teenage mother was completely overshadowed by the joy that she brought to our house.

Even my brother Elijah took on uncle duties, so we were kind of like a family again. It was a mild Spring Day in March of '98 when all of that changed.

I was up getting ready to take my daughter to daycare and go to work at the bank branch that I had only been at a week. My mother had been sick for about two weeks, and had been to the doctor a few times, but had never been hospitalized. She had been off work, and I had taken on some of the duties of housework and chores at home.

It was Monday, March 23$^{rd}$. I woke up to find my mother looking disoriented and trying to dress for work. I told her I didn't think she was well enough to go. Her speech was a little slurred, but she was still trying to talk.

I called my brother, who was also getting ready for work, into the room. Then we called our daddy at work. He told me over the phone that she hadn't looked good before he left, but she had told him to go on. He hung up the phone and headed home. Momma told us that she had not eaten anything that morning, so my brother made her a peanut butter and jelly sandwich, which she tried to eat.

She had already called her friend and co-worker, Peter, to pick up a prescription for her and bring it to our house, but by the time he got there, my daddy was there, and we just took the meds and thanked him.

In the course of all of this, we ended up calling the ambulance, and by the time they arrived, they had to revive her. The last time I saw her alive was when they were loading her into the ambulance.

I rode with Elijah to the hospital after I dropped my baby off at daycare. She was two at the time. Elijah had called his girlfriend then, Brianna (my boo), and I was working to get hold of Tony, who at this time was hustling 24/7, basically living at the dope house on 29th.

We had contacted my mother's best friend, and we were all in the hospital chapel waiting to get word of her condition.

I don't know much about hospitals, but I did know that most families wait in the emergency room with the other families, so I knew that this probably wasn't going to end well. I had gotten in touch with Tony, and Brianna took me home to get my car. I picked Tony up so he could be at the hospital with me.

When I made it back to the hospital and into the chapel, I took one look at my daddy and knew that she was gone.

I don't remember what I did. I'm sure I've blocked it out, as I tend to do when things are too emotional for me to process. I am sure that I broke down and cried.

After they cleaned her up, they allowed us to go in to see her. There she was. My mother, my rock, my world, lying on a hospital table, gone.

--------

The weeks that followed were a blur. There was a multitude of family and friends, numerous flowers, cards and calls offering condolences, food and planning for the funeral, state dignitaries who were honoring my mother, and white and black people alike who had never been to our home, stopping by to bring food and flowers.

There was the Treasurer of the State of Arkansas picking me up and taking me to buy my dress for the funeral. There was a declaration in the newspaper, along with a full obituary, chronicling my mom's contributions to the community, and her thirty-plus years in State government. The State Capital, where she had worked for twenty-plus years, flew their flags at half-staff as a memorial to her, and there I was, along with my favorite aunt, going to the funeral home to dress and groom my mother properly.

There was me being the rock for my daddy while my brother disappeared into himself. There was Tony, making up for the time that he was absent when my grandmother passed, being there and supportive.

There was my first panic attack ever, while I was driving home one night on the freeway. There was Tony proposing to me and promising to take care of me and our daughter. There was a beautiful home-going service, with a church packed full of people of all races and colors.

There was my daddy and my daughter up dancing during one of the many beautiful songs during the service. There was my brother Elijah, always the comedian, cracking jokes about some of our family members during the service. There was the burial at the cemetery down the street from my father's church. There was the repast with family and friends at our home the night of the funeral.

And then... there was nothing.

# Epilogue
## (Trinity) Success

So here I am all 'growed up' or as the kids say, 'glowed up.' It took several tragedies, losses and lots of prayer to make it through, but I was finally seeing myself on the other side.

You know, the thing about success is that it really kind of sneaks up on most of us. You keep putting one foot in front of the other and the next thing you know, you've notched a few wins and accomplished a few goals, and you're known as 'successful.'

Back during my struggle-days, when I was a young mother going to school, dealing with grief and loss, and co-existing with a husband who wasn't the least bit interested in marriage or a family, I would often wonder what it would feel like to achieve the so-called American Dream. To become successful.

I remember talking to a much older friend, whom I deemed successful. He owned his own catering company, after working several years and retiring. He owned his own home, a nice vehicle, and seemed to have money for some of the extras in life. The words he spoke to me when I asked what success looks and feels like have stuck with me to this day.

He said, "Trinity, money and success don't change you. You are still the same you that you've always been. It changes other people's perception of you."

Often in life we have these little 'ah-hah' moments, and for me, that was one of them. I understood clearly what he was saying. Who we are, whether we have success or not, is determined by who we choose to be. That's the only thing that really matters.

I knew from a young age that I didn't want to live my life based on other's perceptions. That little pep talk cleared the way for me to just concentrate on what success was for me. In a nutshell, that meant finishing school (check), raising my children to be healthy (check), well-mannered (check) and independent thinkers (check), having a career that gave me purpose (check), and having a few coins in the bank (amen). That was my definition of success.

I'd had some other bonus successes as well; good friends, strong networks and ties in my field and my community, clients who thought highly of my services, and my own businesses and programs, to name a few. Yeah, I was a modern-day Renaissance Woman.

I had achieved more than my fair share. Forty acres and a mule where?

I had surpassed the dreams of my parents and their parents' parents. American Dream, here I am, a Strong Black Woman! Hear me roar!... and all that jazz.

In spite of possessing all of those things, I could never quiet this pesky feeling of emptiness. I mean, I'm a therapist, for goodness sake, so I had strategies to manage the pains, the heartaches and the disappointments. Unlike some others, I actually subscribe to my own brand of bullshit.

I've always felt like 'if it's good enough for a client, then it's good enough for me.' Thinking this way is probably what has contributed to much of my success. I have always viewed, judged, and cared for others the same as myself. No better and no worse. That type of character goes far in this field, so I have fared well.

Ok. Back to this emptiness hang-up.

For the woman who seemingly has it all - the education, the career, the family - I couldn't avoid the nagging void that always lay just below the surface. But when you have others around you who are in far worse conditions, how can you complain? Who can you talk to about that? For me the answer was no one.

I'd even feel silly talking to myself about it. *Like girl, really? Get it together, self. You've seen way worse days than these.*

And guess what. I was right. I had seen some pretty dark days, so this was a piece of cake. I could push my feelings right on down and keep going. I had mastered this art quite well.

I'm an expert at tucking my feelings in my pocket. That probably helps me as a therapist too, although I wouldn't advise my clients to make a habit of it.

For me, it's been a natural adaptation in my life that I learned way before I could spell the word 'therapist,' let alone expect to become one.

But as a trained clinician, I've learned that it's not always healthy to swallow your feelings, so instead, I've grown fond of journaling. For the majority of my 'successful' years, the Lord and my journal have been my therapists.

---------

In treatment, we often help our clients figure out various coping methods to deal with the tragedies and traumas in their lives. Because face it (therapist hat off), some shit is just horribly fucked up, and no words can fill the empty spaces in your heart.

So (therapist hat back on), we learn ways to cope with life's issues, either in healthy ways (positive coping skills) or unhealthy ways (maladaptive behaviors).

In a nutshell, it means it's not *that* you go through what you go through in life, it's *how* you get through what you go through that makes the difference.

For me, it's been journaling the majority of my thoughts and feelings, talking things through with concerned friends, praying, and remaining active in social activities to exercise the greater humanitarian efforts (positive coping skills).

On occasion, there have been melt-downs, a few tantrums, bags and bags of sunflower seeds eaten, and some release of my frustrations in a sexual way in my marriage (maladaptive behaviors).

Although I had never stepped outside of my marriage, despite all of the issues we had, I often used sex within the marriage as my personal release. I know that's not necessarily a bad thing, but even good things can be a hinderance, if used in a negative way.

That's a topic for another day. Another book, perhaps…

Outside of this catalogue of minor questionable tendencies, I'd say I'm pretty well adjusted to this new life called success.

All is now well in Trinity's world.

But as we know, Truth always has a way of revealing itself, whether we are ready or not.

## About the Author

V. P. Taylor is a professional on a mission to normalize hope, healing, and the idea of community mental wellness. She strives to lift the stigmas that have plagued our community as it relates to mental health and wellness and encourage individual as well as community growth and development.

## Discussion Questions

1. Do you believe in soulmates? If so, do you believe they are meant to be together?
2. Do you think first love ever dies? If so, is it okay to pursue or should the best stay in the past?
3. Why do you believe Truth connected his chances of changing his life so much to Trinity?
4. Have you ever run from love? If so, does it always end up catching you?
5. Do you think Trinity would have gone as far with Truth as she did if her and Tony's marriage was in a happier place.
6. Should all women have a "hoe" phase before they settle down?
7. What are so you think about Trinity wanting the intimate connection with Truth and him holding back that part in the relationship? Was he testing her? himself?
8. Why do you think Trinity was so willing to being a physical relationship with Truth? Do you think women view intimacy different from men?
9. Do you think the intimacy was the beginning or the end of Trinity and Truth's story?
10. Is it okay to cheat on a partner if they have been unfaithful to you?

# YOUR STORY MATTERS

Butterfly Typeface Publishing

www.butterflytypeface.com